THE GAMES PEOPLE PLAY

An Arizona Wine Country Mystery

BY

SUZANNE FLOYD

COPYRIGHT

This is a work of fiction. All characters in this book have no existence outside the imagination of the author. The town of New Haven is a composite of many small towns anywhere.

Cover by Bella Media Management

This book is dedicated to my husband Paul and our daughters, Camala and Shannon, and all my family. Thanks for all your support and encouragement. I love you.

"Once Lost, now found. Eternally thankful!" Our Daily Bread

CHAPTER ONE

The flu season came early and it came hard this year. The ER had been flooded with patients having flu-related problems. Cots lined the halls with patients waiting for an empty bed. It didn't look like there was going to be any relief for a while.

After a crazy morning, I took the opportunity to sit down and rest my feet during a temporary lull. An involuntary sigh of relief escaped my lips as I sank down in the chair. It had been nonstop since I came on shift four hours ago. Closing my eyes, I reviewed the cases we'd already had.

I popped back up moments later at the softly purring voice to see if someone was playing a trick on me. "Hi, Robbie." I quickly sat back down, hoping no one saw me. This was no joke, it was serious. Rob Blake, a nursing assistant, was standing at the counter with his back to me. Shirley Morgan was pressed against him. She had him pinned to the counter, and was moving seductively. Her whispered voice was soft, but not so soft that I couldn't hear her every word.

I peeked around the monitor, hoping they wouldn't be able to see me if they looked my way. I didn't want to watch, but I couldn't look away either. It was like passing a car accident on the highway; you didn't want to see the injured people, but you couldn't stop yourself from looking.

"Come on, Robbie," she purred. "Meet me in the supply closet in five minutes. You know you want to. We can do this. No one will ever know."

"No, Shirley. I told you I'm not going to do it. I have a girlfriend. You have to leave me alone."

"What does one thing have to do with the other? I'm not asking you to marry me." She gave a sexy laugh.

"I'm not going to do it," he repeated. He was getting agitated, struggling to get away from her. "It's not going to happen." I slouched further down in the chair so he wouldn't see me when he turned to face her. This conversation was embarrassing, but it would be even more so if they saw me. He gripped her shoulders to move her away.

"Sure it is. You want a nursing position here when you graduate in a couple of months. This is the way to make that happen. Or not." She lifted one shoulder in a shrug. A gasp escaped my lips, and my mouth dropped open. She was blatantly threatening his job.

Shirley and Rob were both relatively new at New Haven's small hospital. She was always friendly, especially with the younger men. But this went beyond friendly.

"What was that?" Rob's voice squeaked. "Stop it, Shirley. We aren't alone."

"I'll see you soon, Robbie." She gave a throaty giggle as she moved down the hall, confident he would do as she wanted. It didn't seem to bother her that someone might have been witness to her actions. I guess she figured she could always threaten someone else's job.

I shrunk down as far as possible hoping Rob wouldn't come looking for me. I was out of luck. "Pattiann, I'm so sorry. How much did you hear?" His face was beet red. He held his breath, waiting for me to answer.

"Enough to know she was threatening your job, and promising something she couldn't do in order to force you to sleep with her."

His breath came out on a whoosh as he released the breath he'd been holding. "Nothing's going to happen. Please don't say anything."

"Rob, she's sexually harassing you. You don't have to put up with this," I whispered, checking to make sure Shirley was out of earshot.

If possible, his face turned even brighter red, but his shoulders sagged in defeat. "It doesn't matter. Please don't say anything."

"Rob, you have to go to Human Resources about this."

"No, I can't do that. I need my job, and I want that nursing position."

"You want it bad enough to let her blackmail you like that?" I couldn't believe him. I guess it wasn't all that uncommon, but the roles were just reversed. It's usually a man doing the harassing.

"Look, Pattiann, just forget it." His voice was harsh. "This is just the way things work. You've heard all the news stories. Even when those young girls told the people who were supposed to protect them, nothing was done. I guess I should just do it, and she'll leave me alone."

"Are you kidding me? Why would you give in to her?" I knew what he was talking about, but I couldn't believe he was willing to let her get away with this.

"Because I want that nursing position. I need it," he stressed.

"Bad enough to let her do this to you?"

"Yes!"

"What she's doing is illegal," I continued to argue. I couldn't believe he was willing to let her get away with something like this.

"I'm sorry, Pattiann. I'm not going to do anything that will jeopardize my chances of getting that job. Just forget what happened."

"I can't do that," I insisted. "What she's doing is against the law."

"Right. I haven't worked here very long, and I'm just a Nursing Assistant. No one is going to take my word over the head nurse. She'll spin it so I came on to her. I can see it now. I'd be the laughing stock in this whole town. No one would believe she had to force me to have sex with her. I need my job. If my girlfriend found out about this, she'd drop me like a hot potato. If her father didn't kill me first," he added with a sigh. "He already hates me."

He raked his fingers through his dark hair, causing it to stand on end. "Just let it go. Please, Pattiann. I don't want to get in trouble. Don't say anything. Please." Giving me a pleading look, he turned away, hurrying off before I could say anything else.

He was probably right. Who would believe that a woman had to force a man to have sex with her? She was pretty. Some would even say she was sexy. He was caught between the proverbial rock and a hard place.

Sexual harassment had been in the news a lot over the past few months. It's usually a man in a position of power harassing a younger woman. You seldom hear of a woman sexually harassing a man unless it's a teacher and a younger student. He was right about one thing though. Most people would think he enjoyed her attention, maybe even initiated the contact.

Much like rape, sexual harassment is about one person having power over another, threatening them with the loss of their job or maybe a promise of advancement at work the way Shirley had. It shouldn't matter if it's a man with the power, or a woman, though.

I was torn whether I should say something, or keep silent as he requested. I didn't want him to lose his job or the chance of the nursing position later. In a one-hospital town there weren't a lot of options for Rob to find another job. The next closest hospital was thirty miles away. That was a long way on the winding roads around New Haven.

I continued the internal debate over what I should do. Going to Human Resources was the logical place to take this information, but would they believe me? Or would they be like so many others, willing to turn a blind eye simply because the roles have been reversed? Would Rob deny what was happening if I reported what I'd heard? If he wouldn't admit what she was doing, I didn't have a chance of being believed.

Why did he think his girlfriend would break up with him if he reported Shirley? Even if he gave in to Shirley's demands, his girlfriend should understand why he did it. I hoped that would be my reaction if I were in her place. Until someone stood up to Shirley, she would continue to get away with this.

When an ambulance pulled up to the bay doors, I had to

put my concern for Rob aside. As long as we kept busy, Shirley wouldn't have time for a secret rendezvous. That would be good for Rob. If he could put her off long enough, she might decide to leave him alone. But then she would turn her attentions on someone else. I could only hope he'd be able to figure a way out of this situation.

I hurried outside to meet the paramedics. When Angelo Martinez pushed open the driver's side door, my heart did a little hiccup. He was married with two kids, but his partner was single. Ty jumped out of the back of the ambulance, pulling a gurney behind him.

Fresh out of the Air Force, Ty Fisher had moved back to New Haven three months ago. He'd been a fire chief and medic, and it hadn't taken him long to be hired on with the county fire department as a paramedic.

"What have we got?" I looked up into a pair of beautiful green eyes that were framed with thick dark lashes. Most women would die to have those lashes. I tried to remain professional, but it wasn't easy.

"Vera Daily, seventy-six." Ty reported. "She's been sick for three days, and is having trouble breathing. It looks like flu-related pneumonia, but I'll let the professionals make that call." She should have come to the hospital when she first started feeling ill. But like so many this season, her symptoms progressed quickly.

He winked at me, a small smile playing around his lips. We'd been dancing around each other since he started with the department. I kept hoping he would get around to doing more than dance though.

"It looks like our patient is in pretty bad shape, folks," Shirley spoke behind me. "I'll handle this one, Pattiann." She dismissed me without looking up.

"Where's my good buddy?" Angelo came out of the supply room after replenishing the ambulance a few minutes later. "We've already gotten another call."

"He's still in with Mrs. Daily."

He gave a bark of laughter. “I’d better go see if I can rescue him.” He strolled off, in no hurry to rescue Ty.

Was I the only one in the hospital that didn’t know what Shirley was up to? I wondered if she’d propositioned Ty. Or maybe some of the other paramedics, I silently added. She couldn’t threaten their jobs, but that probably wouldn’t stop her from trying.

“Thanks, Buddy.” Ty slapped Angelo on the back, giving a sigh of relief as he stepped out of the exam room. I was still at the desk, and he stopped for a second. “How are things here?”

“It’s been a busy morning. How’s she doing?” I nodded towards the examine room. We’d been fortunate that none of the patients coming into our hospital had died this season. Hopefully, Mrs. Daily hadn’t waited too long before calling for help.

“I think we got her here in time.” He looked back as an X-Ray tech pushed the portable X-Ray machine into the room he’d just left. “Too many people have been waiting too long.” He looked out the door where Angelo had the motor running in the ambulance. “I’d better get out there before he leaves me behind.” He laughed. “I’ll call you?” He phrased it as a question, and I nodded my head.

“He’s one fine male specimen.” I jumped at the voice right behind me. Whirling around, I saw Shirley was watching as Ty stepped up into the waiting ambulance. “I wonder why firemen are always so good-looking. I would love to have some of them working here.” She gave a shiver of anticipatory delight.

I’m sure you would, I thought. She’d try to get every one of them in the supply closet with her. A spike of jealousy shot through me at the thought of her with Ty. I had to give myself a mental shake over that reaction. We hadn’t even gone out on a date yet. I had no reason to be jealous or possessive.

Unaware of where my thoughts had gone, she continued. “It seems that half the male population goes to seed after they reach thirty." She shook her head at that thought. "It would be a shame if those good-looking guys let that happen to them." She ambled off before I could think of an appropriate comeback.

Stepping into the break room for a snack between patients later in the day, I stopped short. Shirley looked up from the papers she was reading. "Hi, Pattiann. How's it going out there?" Her smile seemed genuine. Hopefully Rob wouldn't tell her I had overheard their conversation. I wasn't sure what her reaction would be.

"Busy as usual, but things have slowed down for the time being." I hoped the lull wouldn't give her time to press Rob into meeting her in the supply closet.

"Great. We can all use a breather." She shook her head, sending a cloud of chestnut-colored hair flying. "This flu season is worse than any I've worked in the past." She turned her attention back to the papers in front of her.

Grabbing my bag of apple slices, I made good my escape. I don't know what I expected her to do to me. Until I figured out whether to report what I'd heard, she had no reason to be mad at me.

It was already getting dark when I stepped outside several hours later. It had been a brutal day. Ty had been back three more times that afternoon. Shirley had been tied up elsewhere each time, but there hadn't been time to visit. Everyone in the medical profession was running full-tilt.

Mrs. Daily and three other patients had been admitted just that day with pneumonia. Working three twelve-hour shifts had left me exhausted. I was looking forward to the next four days off.

One good thing came from the heavy patient load. Shirley was kept so busy she hadn't been able to force Rob into meeting for her little tryst. I was still wrestling with what I should do. Rob was right about one thing. Too many times the person being harassed was fired or transferred, while the harasser got away with the crime. I didn't know why that was allowed to happen.

"Phew," Bonnie Carson swept the back of her hand across her forehead as though wiping away sweat. "This has been some week. It's time to relax away from all the tension and drama floating around."

I was unsure if she was talking about the heavy patient load, or something else. How many people knew what Shirley was up to?

"It's still early. How about going to happy hour at The Lamplighter with me, Pattiann?"

"Sorry, Bonnie," I gave my head a tired shake. "It's been a hard day, and a long week." I felt more like sixty-five than twenty-five next to her. She was like the energizer bunny. She never ran down.

"I'm going to pick up something to eat at The Roadside Café, prop my feet up in front of the television, and veg out for a while. It's going to be a busy weekend at the winery." My sister-in-law, Skylar Bishop Wilkinson, owned Sky Vineyards. On my days off I enjoyed helping her out, especially in the tasting room.

"You don't have to work there," she pouted. "I'll bet a certain good-looking paramedic will be at The Lamplighter." She gave me a teasing smile. "You'll forget all about being tired when you see him."

I was grateful it was dark enough to hide the blush I could feel creeping up my face. I thought I'd been a little more discrete about my attraction than that. "Sorry to disappoint you again, but Ty is on shift tonight." She was probably right though. If I thought Ty would be there, I'd agree to go just to see him. I was still hoping he'd ask me out. We'd shared lunch a couple of times, but so far we hadn't managed to have an actual date.

Bonnie knew when she was defeated. "All right," she gave a pitiful sigh. "I guess I'll go by myself." She looked at me to see if I'd cave. I laughed at her theatrics, but sobered quickly enough.

"Don't go alone," I warned. "It isn't safe. You don't know what can happen to a single girl in a bar." As the sheriff of our small county, and even before that as a deputy in northern Arizona, my older brother has told many horror stories of what could happen to women who go to a bar alone.

"But if you won't go with me, I don't have anyone else to go with. Besides," she scoffed, "nothing bad or exciting happens in small towns. The sidewalks roll up at dark around here." She had graduated from nursing school six months ago, and was still trying to make friends. She also wanted some excitement. She'd picked the wrong town for that. New Haven didn't have much of a night life.

I didn't know much about her background, but I knew her parents had been very controlling. This was her first taste of freedom. She wanted to do all the things she thought she'd missed in high school and college. I was afraid she was going to go overboard, and end up in trouble.

"Just because this is a small town doesn't guarantee safety," I warned. "Bad things can happen anywhere." My thoughts returned to the situation Rob found himself in. He certainly didn't feel safe in his current work environment. I turned back to Bonnie. "Why don't you come out to Sky Vineyards with me this weekend? Or try one of the other wineries. They can all use help on festival weekends."

"I don't know anything about wine." She was pouting now.

I leaned tiredly against the side of my car. "You never will if you don't make an effort to learn." I clicked the key fob, unlocking my car door. "Stop by. Tourists pour into the region every weekend. It gets crazy when one of the wineries has a festival. You might even meet a handsome stranger."

Most of the locals visited the different tasting rooms when they needed to replenish their own wine supply, or when they had out-of-town company. Maybe I could interest Bonnie in getting involved at one of the different wineries. It would give her something different to think about, and keep her out of trouble.

"And he'll leave town before I can even give him my name. The only single men in this town are under eighteen or over thirty-five."

"That isn't true, and you know it," I laughed. "There are a lot of nice, single men in town. A bar isn't the place to look for Mr. Right. Come to church with me on Sunday," I suggested. "There are several single men in the congregation."

She sighed. "I'll think about it. My folks weren't much on going to church."

"You might find you like going. We have a great pastor."

"Okay, okay, I'll think about it." She headed for her car.

"Promise me you won't go to The Lamplighter alone," I called after her.

"I promise." Her words floated back to me.

I kept watch in my rearview mirror as she pulled out of the lot behind me. If she decided to stop at The Lamplighter, I'd go after her. When she drove past the local watering hole, I breathed a sigh of relief. Now if she would only join me at Sky Vineyards over the weekend, maybe I could interest her in something other than bar hopping.

CHAPTER TWO

There were only a few cars and pickups in the parking lot of The Roadside Café when I pulled in. That was fine with me. I wouldn't have to wait long for my food. My plan was to pick up a sandwich and head home. I was looking forward to kicking back and putting my feet up.

"Hey, Pattiann." Chase Templeton was sitting at one of the few tables currently occupied.

"Hi, Chase." I walked further into the café. Skylar and Chase have had a semi-friendly competition bordering on open warfare at times since she moved to New Haven a number of years ago. But that didn't mean I had to be rude. There were times when I sensed something sad and lonely about him. Because of the rivalry between them I thought Skylar had overlooked that.

He stood up as I approached. There was a broad smile on his handsome face. "Are you just getting off work? How about joining me?" he asked when I gave a tired nod.

"Thank you, but no, I'm just getting something to take home. It's been a long day. A long week," I added. I was ready to drop.

"Aw, come on," he teased. "I promise not to bite. You'll be able to eat quicker if you stay here." I still hesitated. My step-father had warned me about Chase. He had an ulterior motive for everything he did. I didn't see how it would be to his advantage if I joined him now though. "If it will make you feel better, we can each pay for our own dinner," he continued teasingly. "Or better still, you can pay for both. At least sit at the same table with me." His grin was almost irresistible.

Giving a mental shrug, I nodded my head. What could it hurt to join him for a few minutes? "All right, since you promise not to bite." It seemed innocent enough, but would Greg and Skylar see it that way? Or would they take it as a betrayal?

As sheriff of our small county, my brother Greg considered any boy or man that I might date needed to be thoroughly vetted before I could go out with him. He had embarrassed me on more than one occasion when he gave a boy the third degree when he came to pick me up. I could imagine what he would have to say about this.

An awkward silence settled over us once we were seated. Chase appeared to be having second thoughts about his invitation for me to join him. I felt like a teenager on my first date, and I didn't know why. Over the past two years, I've seen Chase on several occasions, so why was I uncomfortable now? We both studied the menu like it was the first time we'd seen it even though I already knew what I was going to order.

It was a relief when the waitress came up to the table, saving us from staring at the menu any longer. "Hi, Pattiann, Chase, are you eating in tonight?" One heavily penciled eyebrow lifted as she gave us the once-over. I could imagine where her thoughts were headed. "You want your usual?" Madge looked at me. She was a fixture at the small café.

I laughed. "I didn't know I was that predictable." Giving the menu another look, I shook my head. "Maybe I'll be brave, and try the BLTA. I've heard good things about the ones here."

Cocking her hip, Madge rested her hand there. "If you ate in more often, you could try some of our other dishes, too. I keep telling you Bruno is a great chef." She turned to Chase. "What can I get you, honey? You don't eat here often enough to have a regular." In her mid-fifties, Madge enjoyed flirting with any man, it didn't matter if they were young, old, or somewhere in between.

Unlike Shirley, she meant nothing by it. She was happily married to the chef. Bruno King had bought the café when he moved from Phoenix, hoping to make a name for himself before moving on to bigger and better things. That was twenty-five years ago. You couldn't pry either of them out of New Haven now.

"That BLTA sounds pretty good. I think I'll give it a try as well." With a wink for Chase, she headed back to the kitchen with our orders. Neither of us had said anything about this being on separate checks. Was that a simple slipup, or had I deliberately failed to mention that fact? I made a mental note to tell her when she brought our food.

Before the silence could stretch out awkwardly again, a familiar figure came out of the kitchen with a big tub of soapy water. "Hi, George." I gave him a big smile. "I didn't know you worked here. Did you quit your job at the hospital?" George Butler worked in the housekeeping department. Everyone knew him to be a gentle giant.

"N-n-n-no, th-th-this is just a p p-part time job." He looked at Chase, ducking his head. "I'll s-s-see you around." He started scrubbing the table where his tub sat, keeping his head down. Because of his stutter, he was shy and never had much to say.

Chase gave a small chuckle. "It appears you know more people in town than I do. I've been so busy getting my vineyard and winery going that I haven't made a lot of friends." It was both an excuse and an explanation.

I shrugged. "I live and work in town. I'm sure you know more people than you realize. You have to come into town for groceries and other supplies."

His face grew pink at that, and he shook his head. "I have a lady come in once a week to clean my place. She brings groceries and fixes several dishes I can pop in the microwave. When I run out of those, I come into town or eat sandwiches."

It was sort of a sad tale, but I understood. Cooking for one and eating alone was the reason I spent so much time at Sky Vineyards on my days off. That's where my family was. But I'd never heard anything about Chase having any family here. "How long have you lived in New Haven?" I realized how little I knew about him. That seemed like a good place to start a conversation.

"About ten years," he didn't elaborate further. The few

other times I'd run into him, he was always full of bluster. Now he appeared reluctant to talk about himself. I wasn't going to let this opportunity to learn a little more about him pass by, though.

"Where are you from originally?"

"Oregon," he stated, pausing before going on. "That's where I got my start in wine making." Again he didn't go into detail. Skylar always said he was so full of himself. Drawing him out now felt like pulling teeth.

"What brought you to Arizona and New Haven?"

He paused for a moment as he considered how much to say. "A clash with my parents," he finally said. "My dad owns a large company in Portland. He expected my brother and me to follow in his footsteps. Working in the different wineries was fine for a summer job, but certainly not something to do with your life."

"What about your brother? Did he go his separate way as well?"

"No, Charles always toed the family line. He was perfectly willing to follow in Dad's footsteps." Bitterness tinged his words. There wasn't just a rift between Chase and his father, but his brother as well. Apparently his bluster and big talk was a cover-up for the hurts inflicted by his family.

"Hopefully your dad has come around to see that this has been a successful career choice for you."

He gave a humorless chuckle. "I'm sure my father doesn't have a clue what I've been doing. It was always his way or the highway." He drew a deep breath, letting it out slowly. "I chose the highway. I left Oregon right after high school. I haven't spoken to him since."

I couldn't imagine being estranged from my family. I'd be lost without the support of my mom and brother. My father had died when I was still young, but I remembered him as being very supportive of anything I wanted to do. "What about your mother? How does she feel about your winery?"

"She tried to encourage me, but she couldn't stand up to

her husband. I'm told she had been an independent thinker when she was younger, but Dad made sure that didn't continue once they were married."

It was obvious now why he had been so bent on expanding his vineyard. Whether he realized it or not, he was still trying to prove himself to his father. Hopefully, his father would see the error of his way before it was too late.

"How did you decide you wanted your vineyard in Arizona? Oregon has a big wine industry as well, doesn't it?" I was asking a lot of personal questions, but I wanted to keep him talking.

He shrugged. "After interning at a vineyard and winery in Australia for two years, I moved back to the states. Staying in Oregon wasn't really an option for me." He didn't elaborate on that cryptic statement. "The wine industry in Arizona was taking off. I wanted to get in on the ground floor, so to speak. Until recently people thought it was too hot and dry here to grow wine grapes. The climate in southern Arizona is compatible to certain varietals, and the land was cheaper than California. I thought it was now or never." He gave another shrug.

Madge interrupted our conversation when she set two plates down on the table. The sandwich and fries filled the big platter-sized plates to overflowing. For the next few minutes the only sound was us devouring our food. When our initial hunger pangs were satisfied, Chase gave me a little smile. I didn't realize how hungry I was until she brought the food. He sat back with a satisfied sigh. "I've done all the talking so far. What brought you to New Haven?"

"My brother Greg. When he moved down here for his job, Mom and I followed." For a second his face tightened at the mention of Greg's name. When Skylar first moved to New Haven, Chase had pictured them combining their wineries and their lives. Skylar wasn't interested in a business relationship or a personal one with him. When Greg swept her off her feet, Chase had taken that as a personal insult. Apparently the rejection of his father had caused a lot of insecurities for him.

Forcing himself to relax, he took another bite out of the sandwich before picking up the conversation again. "Have you always lived in Arizona?"

"Born and raised," I confirmed with a laugh. "My mom was raised here as well. We lived in Tempe until Greg started college in Flagstaff. Mom and I moved up there so that we were close. That's where I went to college as well. When Greg got the job with the sheriff's department down here, we followed him again. We both have jobs that allow us to work almost anywhere."

"Sounds like you're all close." A sad expression crossed his handsome face for a brief second. "New Haven is a lot smaller than Tempe or Flagstaff. How do you like small town life? There isn't much of a night life here." He echoed Bonnie's complaint, but it didn't seem to matter to him.

"It's different, but I'm adaptable." I shrugged. "I've never been a party girl so the lack of a night life doesn't bother me."

"You and your brother have different last names. There must be a story there."

"Yes, Mom has been widowed twice. After my dad died, she vowed never to get married again. That was before she met Joe of course," I added with a laugh. "It was love at first sight for both of them."

This was beginning to feel like a real date as we asked the normal first date questions. I wasn't sure how I felt about that. Joe wouldn't be happy. His opinion of Chase hadn't improved much since Skylar and Greg were married. We weren't in a hurry to leave though. The exhaustion I'd been feeling earlier had disappeared. There were more customers in the dining room, but no one was waiting to be seated, so there was no need to rush.

Yawning for the third time, my face began to heat up. "I'm sorry, Chase, but I really need to get home." Looking at my watch I was surprised at how long we'd been sitting there. I was also surprised by how enjoyable the evening had been.

"It's been a long week, and I'm helping Sky out at her winery this weekend."

"If you get tired of working for your sister-in-law, I'm always looking for someone to help out at my place," he suggested with a sly smile.

"Um, I don't think that would go over very well with some of my family," I laughed. Especially Joe, I thought, keeping that to myself.

"It's just a suggestion," he shrugged. "Can't blame me for trying."

"I have a friend who might be interested in helping out in your tasting room. I'll bring her by some time. She's new to the area, and needs something to keep her busy on our long weekends from the hospital."

Sensing we were getting ready to leave, Madge came over with the check. "Split check, remember," I said when he took the slip she placed on the table.

Chase shook his head. "I lied." He chuckled. "I don't get out much, and I've really enjoyed tonight." Giving in gracefully was my only out. Besides, I had enjoyed the evening as well.

Following me outside, he walked me to my car and opened the door for me when I clicked the remote. "I'll see you around. Thanks again for joining me. It was nice having company for a change." He stood back, watching as I pulled out of the lot before going to his big truck.

CHAPTER THREE

Standing at the window of his second floor hotel room, he stared down at the dusty town below. Who in their right mind would choose to live here? he wondered. But that was the problem. That boy hadn't been in his right mind since he was small. The blame for that could be laid at his mother's feet, he thought. She indulged him with everything he ever wanted, big or small.

Winemaking had become a big business in recent years. It might be something that would fit in with his plan for growth. He didn't understand why the boy kept his operation so small. By now he should have gone national, instead of remaining simply a regional winery. He should be looking to expand. What he had wasn't a business, it was a hobby. If he wanted to continue making wine, he needed to take it to the next level. If he didn't have the guts to make the move, he would do it for him.

~~~

After putting a load of clothes in the washing machine and cleaning the kitchen, I headed for the shower. I wanted to wash the hospital smell out of my hair. I tried to do one household chore each evening. That freed up my days off to work with Sky at her vineyard, or go shopping in Tucson. It was later than usual, but I had enjoyed the evening with Chase.

My heart jumped into my throat when someone began pounding on my door. It was too late for visitors. Something had to be wrong. After checking the security peep hole, I opened the door. "Are you all right, George? What happened?" I didn't see any blood, so I assumed he wasn't injured. Why was he at my house, especially so late at night?

His breath came out in a whoosh like he'd been holding it for a long time. His big stature seemed to sag with the sigh. "I th-th-thought s-s-s-something bad was g-g-going t-t-to
~~~

happened t t to you when th-th-that g-g-guy f-f-followed you." His stutter was worse when he was agitated or upset.

"Slow down, George," I said calmly. "What guy? Are you talking about Chase, the man I was with at the diner?" I clarified when he looked puzzled.

His answer didn't agree with the head shake. "M-m-maybe, sort of." He looked confused now.

"Take a breath, so I can understand you."

He followed my instructions, drawing a deep breath. "Someone followed you." Talking in a sing-song voice the stutter was almost gone. "I was afraid he was going to hurt you." His face grew hot with that. "I couldn't leave the diner until now."

My breath hitched in my throat. "Do you know who followed me?" His shoulders slumped, and he shook his head this time. "Well, maybe it was another customer leaving at the same time I did." While Chase and I had been talking several other people had come in. I hadn't noticed if they left the same time we had. "Maybe it was someone from another business," I added hopefully.

He shrugged. "I j-j-j-just wanted to m-m-make s-s-sure you were okay." He was nervous again, and his face turned pink in the porch light. Before I could say anything, he turned, hurrying to the old car sitting at the curb.

Because of his stutter few people took him seriously. But the nurses knew that if something was broken all we had to do was call George. He would have it fixed in no time. There wasn't anything outside of medical equipment that he couldn't fix. Given time and the right instructions, I felt certain he would be able to fix that as well.

"Thank you for checking on me," I called, but I wasn't sure he heard me. A chill that had nothing to do with the cool night air swept down my spine. Had someone really followed me home? A strange car was parked in front of a neighbor's house, but I couldn't tell if anyone was inside. I quickly closed the door, twisting the key on the dead bolt lock.

There were several small businesses close to the diner. It must have been someone from one of those leaving at the same time I had. Maybe if I told myself that often enough, I'd believe it.

I'd heard all the horror stories of women turning up missing after leaving a bar alone. But The Roadside Café wasn't a bar, I reminded myself. They served drinks, but no one sat around for hours drinking until they were drunk.

New Haven was a quiet little town. There wasn't a lot of crime. The border with Mexico was close by, and occasionally there was trouble with drug and people smugglers. But that was mostly out in the desert, not here in town. Illegals wanted to stay away from the smaller town where they would be easily noticed. They made their way to the more populated areas where they could blend in.

I spent a restless night, and was still spooked the next morning. I decided to leave grocery shopping for another day as I headed out to Sky Vineyards. It was still early, and the morning air still held a chill. Before the day was over, the temperature would reach into the eighties.

"Hey kiddo, you're a little early." Joe came out of the barn. Bending down, he placed a kiss on my cheek. "You look tired. Rough week?"

"You could say that. There are a lot of people sick this flu season. Did you get your flu shot like I told you to?" I tipped my head to one side, looking up at him through my lashes.

"Now don't start in on me again. Never had one of them shots, and I'm not going to start now. I haven't been sick more than one day in the last fifty years. Why should this year be any different?"

We'd had this discussion several times in the past month. Joe wasn't big on doctors. "You never know when someone just coming down with the flu might come into the tasting room."

"Good reason not to spend much time with a bunch of strange folks." He placed another kiss on my cheek, heading out to the vineyard. That was his territory. He spent most of his time working there.

I shook my head. He wasn't much for long conversations either. Mom did enough talking for both of them. Skylar poked her head out the big doors. "You coming inside to work, or just standing around looking at things?"

"Coming, boss. You're such a slave driver," I joked. It didn't matter what time of year it was, there was always work to be done in the winery. Several different wines would soon be ready for bottling. I enjoyed helping with that process.

I wasn't going to say anything about the possibility that someone had followed me home the night before. George might have jumped to the wrong conclusions when someone simply left the parking lot the same time I did.

When Becky Daniels' older model car pulled up to the double doors, she jumped out as it rocked to a halt. She worked part time in the tasting room, but it wasn't open today. Her worried expression gave both of us cause for concern.

"Sky, someone is trying to buy up the vineyards around here." Her words tumbled out on top of each other.

"Slow down. What are you talking about?" Sky propelled her over to a bench where she could sit down.

Drawing a couple of deep breaths, Becky started again. "A real estate agent showed up at McMahan Vineyard this morning. He said he's looking to buy several vineyards for a client."

"Several vineyards?" Skylar and I spoke at the same time. "Who's his client?" Skylar finished.

She shook her head. "It's supposed to be confidential. His offer was good. A little over the top, if you ask me. Jim was afraid Mike and Cyndi would take him up on the offer, it was that good. He really enjoys working for them." Jim is Betsy's husband. After a career in the military, they had decided to settle down in New Haven.

"That winery has been their dream for a long time. They wouldn't accept any offer no matter how good it is." Skylar frowned. "There are a couple of the newer owners who might jump at a good offer though."

"That's what Cyndi said," Becky agreed. "Mike thought we should spread the word to the other owners though. He said the guy was sort of pushy."

"I appreciate you letting me know." Worry drew her brows together over troubled eyes. When I first met Skylar and Joe someone had targeted her for revenge against her father. He had tried to ruin Sky Vineyards. He even tried to sell the winery without her knowledge. He was in jail awaiting trial for fraud, identity theft, and murder.

Becky had only been gone a short time when a fancy car pulled into the lane leading up to the tasting room. It didn't take much guesswork to know who he was and what he wanted.

Most people who come to the wine country of southern Arizona don't bother dressing up. This guy was the exception. His suit probably cost more than my entire wardrobe. I followed Skylar outside. Something about him said *shady lawyer*.

"Hello, ladies, how are you this fine day?" A big, oily smile spread across his clean-shaven face. He offered his hand to each of us. Squeezing my hand, he pumped his arm up and down hard enough to make my teeth rattle. When he dropped my hand, I wiggled my fingers to make sure they still worked.

"What can I do for you?" Sky asked. There was a chill in her voice.

"I have a client who is interested in buying a vineyard." He handed her a business card. Barely glancing at it, she handed it to me. *Samuel Earnhardt, Attorney at Law.* My guess was correct, but I thought Becky said a realtor had been at McMahan Vineyards. Were two people trying to buy up the vineyards?

"I'm sorry, sir, but I don't know of any vineyards for sale around here." She cut him off before he could say anything more. "I'm very busy right now, so you'll have to excuse me."

"You haven't heard the offer yet." If he said 'an offer you can't refuse' I was going to call Greg. My cell phone was already in my hand.

"It doesn't matter what your offer is. I'm not interested in selling."

"Everything has a price."

"Not anything of mine." Her temper was beginning to heat up. "Who would make an offer to buy something that isn't for sale?"

"My client prefers to remain anonymous." He was straining to keep his smile in place.

"Well, you can tell your anonymous client that I'm not interested no matter how lucrative the offer is. Now, I would like you to leave."

His smile slipped a little further. "It would be in your best interest to hear me out."

"That sounds pretty close to a threat." Her hands were balled into fists now. She would defend what was hers, no matter what.

"Nothing of the sort. If you will just listen to what I have to say, you might be interested."

"I doubt that. Now leave before I call the sheriff." We were both holding our cell phones now.

"That is unnecessary. I'm here to make a legitimate offer. There is no need to involve the sheriff."

"What's going on here?" Joe must have seen the car from the field as it pulled into the lane. I was grateful for his presence now. He kept his dark gaze on our unwanted visitor when he addressed Skylar. Even Cody, Sky's Golden Retriever, had come out to join us. As the tasting room's official greeter, I wasn't sure how much protection he would be. He might lick the man to death though.

"I was just telling this *gentleman* that we're not interested in selling our property." Joe looked out towards the road for a realtor's sign. When he didn't find one his frown grew even darker.

Mr. Earnhardt had the good sense to take a step away from Joe. “Now there’s no need to get upset. I was just telling Miss Bishop here that I have a client interested in buying her vineyard. It would be in her best interest…” He didn’t finish his sentence when Joe took a step closer to him.

“I’d stop right there if I were you,” Joe growled. “It’s in yer best interest to get off our land and not come back. No one in these parts is interested in selling.”

I wondered if that was entirely true. Skylar said some of the newer owners might be willing to sell if his offer was as lucrative as he said. It took five years or longer before you could begin making wine from new vines. Until then, you had to buy grapes from other vineyards. Unless they were prepared for that, it could take a big bite out of any savings.

I hoped no one would sell to this guy’s anonymous client. Anyone who would send a lawyer with the type of message delivered here wouldn’t be a good neighbor or competitor.

Taking Joe’s implied threat seriously, Mr. Earnhardt hurried to his fancy car. Gravel spun beneath the tires as he sped down the lane. We gave a collective sigh once the big car was out of sight.

“If he’s legit, we need to figure out who’s behind this offer and why,” Joe said. “You best let the other owners know he might be paying them a visit. Legit or not, we don’t want someone pulling a fast one.” This was a long speech for him. He was worried about another problem like the one they’d had not so long ago.

“It appears we have a lawyer and a realtor anxious to buy up some wineries,” Skylar said, filling him in on Becky’s visit.

We spent the rest of the day racking the barrels to remove the sediment left in the bottom after the wine had been removed. It was hard work, but it helped take our minds off someone trying to buy up the local vineyards. We were both hot and sweaty by the end of the day.

~~~

Reading the caller ID on his phone before answering, he
~~~

groaned. The man was going to drive him nuts before this was over. Putting on what he hoped was a professional tone, he pressed the connect button.

"How did things go today?" Anxious to get things started, the caller spoke before he could say anything.

"I stopped at three vineyards." He paused, taking a deep breath.

"Only three? Why not more? What did they think of your offer?"

"These people are pretty committed to what they're doing. It might be easier to buy up some vacant land, and plant your own vines." He held his breath. This wasn't what his client wanted to hear.

"I didn't ask for your opinion or advice. I'm not interested in buying vacant land and starting over." He planned on buying as many vineyards that were already operational as he could. He could always pay someone to run them. But making wine wasn't his objective here. He had other plans.

"I expected more from someone with your reputation," he continued to rant. "There are more than three vineyards in the area. Why haven't you talked to more than that?"

"By the time I made it to the third place, they already knew I was coming. If people don't want to sell, they aren't interested in talking to a lawyer."

"Then maybe I need to find one with some fire in his belly."

"I thought I'd go to a couple of the newer wineries tomorrow. They would be more interested in listening to an offer."

"I gave you a list of the wineries to go to, and a new startup was far down on that list. Where did you go?"

He gulped hard. He'd been hoping to avoid that question. "Sky Vineyards," he said, waiting for the explosion. When it didn't come, he continued. "She wouldn't listen to the offer. She's pretty stubborn. I'll try again when she has a chance to think things over."

"Think things over? What the hell are you talking about?" The voice coming through the phone line was all the more menacing for its softness. "I told you to stay away from her for now. What exactly did you tell her?"

"I told her what you wanted me to say, that I had an offer for her vineyard she should listen to." He bristled, but held on to his temper. This client liked running the show.

"I told you to finesse those people, not threaten them. For a big-time lawyer, you're sounding more like a country bumpkin."

"You said you wanted to buy her vineyard, that's what I was trying to accomplish. If she isn't interested at this time, there will be others who will be."

"I don't want just her *vineyard, I want them all. I told you she was going to be a hard sell. After what happened last year, she's naturally going to be suspicious. You should have listened to me and started with one of the other owners."*

"She might be the hardest one to get to come to terms, but it would also make the others fall in line if she agreed to sell. They'll follow her lead," he argued.

"How did that work out for you? Stop acting like a Mafia don right out of the movies. I gave you the list of vineyards you were to target, so get this done."

"If you don't like the way I'm doing this, maybe you should approach these people yourself. You know them. They would be more receptive to you than a stranger." He didn't want to lose this client, but he was getting tired of his heavy-handed approach.

"My reasons for doing things are none of your business. It's your job to follow orders to the letter and not ask questions. Do you understand?"

"Yes." He gulped out the word, but the line was already dead.

His first inclination was to throw the phone across the room, but it wouldn't do any good. This was the first job he'd done for this client. If he could accomplish this one task, it could turn out to be very profitable for him. The billable hours alone were worth putting up with the high opinion the man had of himself. With his attitude, it was no wonder he wanted someone else to handle things for him. No one wanted to do business with him. It was a miracle he managed to stay in business if he treated his customers the way he treated someone working for his best interests.

He'd start fresh in the morning with another owner. There were bound to be several on the list willing to sell for a big pay day. After all, how profitable could all these wineries be? This was the desert, not Italy or France. Hell, it wasn't even California. Small boutique wineries and craft breweries were the up and coming thing. They were sprouting up all over the place. With so many in one area, how lucrative could they be?

The man was right about one thing though. It wasn't his business what he was going to do with all of the wineries once he obtained them. He didn't really care as long as he got paid.

CHAPTER FOUR

"Aren't you staying for dinner?" Mom asked. She had only been home a few minutes when I was ready to head back to town. On my days off, I usually stay for dinner. But I wanted to get home before dark. The possibility of someone following me the night before still had me spooked.

I wasn't going to mention that though. That would mean I would have to explain about having dinner with Chase, and I didn't even want to go there. I was hoping he would be as discreet when Skylar went over to talk to him about the lawyer. I kept telling myself George had been mistaken the night before, but it wasn't helping.

"I'm sorry, Mom, not tonight. It was a crazy week, and I'm bone tired. I still have some laundry to do before I can fall into bed." That was the truth, just not all of it. "I promise I'll stay tomorrow night. I'll even make dinner for all of us."

Being the only one not part of a couple, I sometimes felt like a third wheel with the two newlywed couples. But that was on me, not them. It would be nice to get her opinion about my dilemma at work though. In spite of Rob's insistence that I keep it to myself, I was still debating whether I should go to HR with what I'd overheard.

Before she could start asking me about my social life, or lack of one, I placed a kiss on her cheek. "I'll see you tomorrow. You'll be here all day on Saturday as well. We can have a real gab fest then, and you can ask me all the embarrassing questions you're dying to ask." We both laughed. I knew her so well. Until I actually had a date with Ty I wasn't going to mention him either.

Chase was sitting on his porch as I drove past. Like most of the owners, he had built his house beside his winery and tasting room. His vineyard was spread out on either side of the buildings. I wanted to ask him if he'd noticed someone follow me the night before, but that would have to wait. I just wanted to go home. It hadn't been a lie when I told Mom it had been a bad week. I was ready to fall into bed.

Until I was safely home with the doors locked, I didn't realize how tense I'd been on the drive. Kicking off my shoes at the door, I flipped on lights as I made my way to the kitchen. Warm days and cool evenings were the norm in southeastern Arizona. I'd worn shorts that morning when I left home. Now I was chilly, and wanted something warm to eat. Eyeing the sparse offerings in my refrigerator, I shook my head. I needed to get groceries soon, or I wouldn't have anything for lunches next week. There wouldn't be anything for dinner when I got home from work either.

First things first, I thought. After a day of racking barrels, I needed a shower. Removing sediment from the barrels was hard work. In spite of the cool evening air, it felt like my clothes were plastered to my body.

Making sure the blinds were all closed, I headed for my bedroom, stripping out of my sweaty clothes as I went. Fifteen minutes later I was back in the kitchen feeling fresh and clean. My hair was still damp from the shower, and I left it to air dry. Pulling open the refrigerator again, I studied the few items there. When my stomach growled, I grabbed the bread and a couple of slices of cheddar cheese. I always kept canned soup in the cupboard. Tomato soup and a grilled cheese sandwich was the perfect cold weather meal.

A noise on the patio caused my heart to jump into my throat, and my stomach to plummet to my toes. Was someone out there? I hadn't seen anyone suspicious following me home. That didn't mean someone wasn't out there now. The doors were locked, and nothing had been disturbed in the house. "Calm down," I admonished myself. "It's just a deer or something."

It wasn't unusual for wild animals like deer, coyotes, even javelins to forage around in town for something to eat. Whatever or whoever was out there, I wasn't going to go out and check. I'd worry about the mess they were making in the morning. Javelins could get pretty nasty when their dinner was interrupted. There wasn't anything for them to eat, which would probably make them even nastier.

~~~

He crouched down under the kitchen window, holding his breath. He'd barely had enough time to go out the back door when she came in the front door. Another minute and she would have walked in on him. He needed to be more careful. This wasn't a job he could hire out.

When the light in the kitchen came on he remained still, afraid of making noise. The light went off almost immediately, but he remained where he was. Waiting another few minutes, his legs began to cramp. Finally deciding it was safe to move away from the house, he stood up.

The kitchen light came on again just as he moved, startling him so he bumped into one of the patio chairs. "Damn," he muttered. He didn't wait around to see if she would come out to investigate. Getting caught this early in his game plan wouldn't be good. There were no fences between the properties, and he made a mad dash across the yard, disappearing into the darkness.

~~~

Trying to put the noise outside from my mind, I sat down in front of the television with my grilled cheese sandwich and a cup of hot tomato soup. I scrolled through the channels for something interesting to watch. When nothing captured my attention, I flipped it off again.

A sense of apprehension settled down on me. I was still trying to decide what to do about Shirley. If Ty and Angelo knew what she was doing, it was reasonable to think the administration was also aware of her actions. So why hadn't they stopped her?

In several big cases recently, the victims had reported the assaults, but nothing had been done about it. Was that the case here? I prayed that Rob wouldn't give in to her threats. He was planning on getting married after he graduated. Even though he had been forced into a bad situation, it wouldn't bode well for a new marriage.

My mind returned to George's visit the night before. Had someone followed me home? Who would do that? What would be the purpose? I stared at the blank television for a long moment but no answers came to me. Telling myself that George had jumped to the wrong conclusion, I picked up my dirty dishes. It was time to think of something else.

After cleaning up and stowing the leftover soup in the refrigerator, I headed to the spare bedroom. I hadn't checked e-mail for several days. Working twelve hours didn't leave much time or energy at the end of each day to do more than grab a bite to eat and crash on the couch with the latest book I was reading.

Mom and I had shared the house before she and Joe got married. After that, I had turned my old room into an office. Along with a day bed, there was a desk for my laptop and a small file cabinet for any important papers. I hadn't been in there in almost a week, but I always put things away when I finished working in there. So why did it look like a tornado had swept through the room now? Papers were scattered across the top of the desk. Files in the drawers had been gone through. Someone had been in here, and it wasn't me.

My heart was pounding in my ears as I went through the house to see what else had been tampered with. Nothing was missing. My television and laptop were still here. My jewelry case hadn't been touched. I kept cash in one drawer, and it was still there. Why would someone break in and not take anything? What could they be looking for? Any sensitive papers I had were locked in a safe deposit box at the bank.

My hands were shaking when I reached for my cell phone. For several minutes I debated who to call. The small town of New Haven didn't have their own police force. We relied on the sheriff's department for any law enforcement needs. Calling the sheriff's office wasn't a good idea. Even if Greg wasn't on duty, he would know I'd reported a possible break-in. His overprotective tendencies would kick in, and he'd expect me to move out to the winery. That would be going backward instead of forward.

Had the noise on the patio really been a wild animal looking for something to eat? Or had someone been out there? Had I interrupted a burglar looking for something to steal? That didn't make sense though. There was nothing of value in the files. Going to the backdoor, I tested the dead bolt lock. My heart jolted in my chest. It wasn't locked.

The last thing I do before going to work is make sure all the doors and windows are locked. Had I been in such a hurry that morning that I forgot to check? I shook my head. Living alone was still relatively new to me. I didn't leave things to chance. I always made sure everything was locked before going anywhere. When I heard the noise out back, I hadn't thought to check the lock on the door. I was becoming too complacent. Greg would have my head if he knew.

That settled the debate raging inside me. What could they do? I argued with myself. Greg had been in law enforcement long enough that I knew the drill. If nothing had been taken, and there was no sign of forced entry, there was nothing they could do. A dead bolt was supposed to be secure, but a professional burglar would be able to pick almost any lock. I'd check the outside lock for any new scratch marks in the morning. I wasn't going outside when it was dark.

Placing a kitchen chair under the door knob on both doors, I went to bed. It was a low-tech form of security, but it would keep someone from picking the lock and getting in. In spite of that, it was another restless night. I jerked awake at every nighttime noise. Getting out of bed at the first sign of dawn, I was as tired as I'd been when I went to bed. After three cups of coffee and a long shower, I was ready to face the day.

Examining the locks as soon as it was light enough to see, I didn't find any sign that they had been tampered with. I checked and rechecked the doors and windows before heading to the grocery store. Everything was locked tight. Would it be that way when I came home? I didn't like being paranoid, and seeing the boogeyman behind every bush.

When I'd checked the patio to see if a wild animal had done any damage the night before, one chair appeared to have been moved. That could account for the sound I'd heard. Nothing else had been disturbed. There were scuff marks in the dust, but an animal could have done that as well. Telling myself that a wild animal had bumped the chair and been scared off wasn't working. What if someone had been out there and accidently knocked into the chair? The door had been unlocked. If they wanted to hurt me, they wouldn't have run off.

It was hard to concentrate on food as I rushed through the store. What would I find when I got home? Locked doors and windows wouldn't stop someone if they really wanted in. It would be easy enough to break a window. My neighbors all worked, so no one would be home to hear the sound of glass breaking.

In spite of my worries, everything was as I left it a short time ago. Quickly putting my groceries away, I used the same low-tech security method I had the night before. That still left one door vulnerable for someone to pick the lock, but there was nothing I could do about that. I said a small prayer for safety, and headed back to my car. I wanted to get to the vineyard before the tasting room opened. It was the first day of the festival. Things could get a little crazy.

A few miles out of town my car coughed and sputtered before it coasted to a stop. "What now?" Greg made sure I took the car in for maintenance on a regular basis. The mechanic at the local auto shop had given it a clean bill of health just three weeks ago. He always told me if there was something wrong so I wouldn't get stranded.

I mentally went over the check list Greg had drilled into my head when I first got my license: oil changed every five thousand miles; transmission and brake fluid checked; proper air pressure in the tires; battery checked. All of that and more had been done. What else could be wrong?

I looked at the gas gauge. The needle was sitting on E. That couldn't be. I'd filled the tank two days ago. I switched the key to off, and turned it back on again. The needle didn't move. Someone had syphoned the gas out of my tank. If there had been any doubt in my mind before, this settled it. Someone really had been in my house the night before. When they didn't have time to steal anything in the house, maybe they came around front, leaving me only enough gas to get to the grocery store and back.

Telling my family that piece of news wouldn't be pretty either. Letting them believe I forgot to get gas wouldn't be much better. I sighed as I reached for my cell phone. Could I let them think this happened in the parking lot at the hospital? That way I wouldn't have to tell them that someone had been in my house. With the phone still in my hand, I debated the pros and cons of putting a different spin on this. I wasn't good at telling lies.

CHAPTER FIVE

When a large pickup pulled up behind my car, my stomach did a little flip flop. In a town the size of New Haven, you know most everyone and they know you. But one truck looked pretty much the same as another to me. With the sun on the windshield, I couldn't see the driver.

The breath I'd been holding came out on a sigh of relief when I recognized the man who stepped out. I didn't have to worry about him doing me harm, but he would play havoc with my heart.

At five-foot-ten with emerald green eyes surrounded by thick lashes any woman would give her arm for, Ty caused heart palpitations in all the nurses when he came into the hospital. He would probably think I'm a total airhead who forgets to put gas in her car. That wasn't the image I wanted him to have of me.

"Well, hello. Are you having car trouble?" A teasing smile tugged at his full lips when I opened the door and stepped out.

Well, duh, did he think I was parked along the road for the fun of it? I kept that thought to myself. "Um, ah, yeah," I hesitated. "I'm out of gas." I bristled slightly when he chuckled. "I filled up two days ago."

He frowned now. "Do you have a leak in your tank?" He leaned down to see if he could spot a leak.

"No, I don't think that's what happened." I didn't want to explain that someone had syphoned the gas out of my tank. Maybe that wasn't so unusual though. "You wouldn't happen to have a spare gallon of gas in the back of your truck, would you? I'm willing to pay for it."

"No, I don't keep a spare gallon with me, but I do have a gas can. I can go get a couple of gallons for you. Are you sure that's all that's wrong with the car?"

"Yes, I'm sure," I sighed. Why did men assume women didn't have a clue about cars? Admittedly, I don't know anything, but he didn't need to take it for granted that I didn't. "I had it in the shop a few weeks ago for all the necessary maintenance. I filled the tank with the proper gas two days ago." I didn't want him to think I would put diesel in instead of regular gas either. I'm not totally incompetent. "I should have plenty of gas, but I don't."

"It's not a comforting thought that someone syphoned the gas out of your car, but it isn't unheard of." He shrugged. "If there were illegals in the area, maybe they needed gas to get to their next stop."

Is that who had been in my house the night before? I liked that idea only slightly better than a local thief preying on our town.

"It won't take more than fifteen minutes to go back and get some gas. Will you be all right out here by yourself, or would you rather go with me?" He seemed to debate which option would be best.

"I'll wait here." I reached for my purse on the front seat.

He waved off the offer of money for the gas. "Stay in the car. If someone you don't know stops, don't get out or roll down your window." Now he was acting like my big brother. Not the attitude a woman wants from a good-looking man.

True to his word, Ty was back fifteen minutes later. "If you're going any distance, you'd better head back to town for gas first," he advised. "Two gallons isn't going to get you very far."

"It isn't far to my sister-in-law's winery," I sighed. "I'll get gas tonight." I wanted to be at the winery before Skylar opened up so I could find out what the other owners had to say the night before.

He nodded his head. "I'll follow you just in case you do have a gas leak." I wasn't going to argue. This would be a good time to get to know him better.

When Ty's big truck followed my car down the lane leading to the winery, Joe came out of the back building. There was a frown on his grizzled face as he looked at Ty when he stepped out of the truck. "You want something?" It wasn't a friendly greeting, but considering the lawyer's visit the day before, I couldn't blame him.

"Joe, this is Ty Fisher. He's a friend of mine." This was the first time I'd brought a man to the winery. I sighed when his bushy brows dropped low over his eyes. I hoped he wouldn't give Ty the third degree the way Greg had done on several occasions in the past.

Joe didn't say anything, waiting for me to give an explanation for Ty being here. "He came to my rescue when I had a little car trouble," I finally said with a sigh. "He just wanted to make sure I got here without any other problems." I was hoping both men would accept my explanation, and let it go. I should have known better.

"Car trouble?" Joe asked. "Didn't you just have the car in for maintenance?"

"Yes, but sometimes these things happen. Ty helped me out. It's no big deal." I gave Ty a warning glance. "This is Joe Barnes, my step-dad, and general protector," I said with a laugh, hoping to put an end to Joe's worried frown.

"It's nice to meet you, Mr. Barnes." Ty held out his hand. Greg always said you could judge a man's character by his handshake. Joe was of the same opinion. I could tell he was sizing Ty up in that brief moment.

"Nice meeting you," Joe nodded his head. I thought that meant Ty had passed muster, but I couldn't be sure. "You not planning on working today?" Joe turned to me. Apparently he wasn't through questioning me in his own shorthand way of talking. His sentences were always short and to the point. It always sounded like words were at a premium, and he didn't want to waste them.

"Sure am, but as long as Ty's here I thought I'd show him around first if Skylar doesn't mind. We still have a little while before opening." I wasn't going to learn what the other owners had to say, but I was okay with that. Any time spent with Ty was a good time.

"Yeah, sure." I wasn't sure what that meant, but I didn't ask either. His lips curled up into his mustache. Maybe he guessed my ulterior motives. I decided to change the subject.

"How's Mom today? I didn't have much time to talk to her last night.

"Keeping busy, maybe too busy," he said, giving his head a shake.

"Is she still enjoying her new position?" She'd been promoted to manager of the small branch bank in New Haven after the former manager had been arrested last year. His trial was still pending while the authorities looked into any number of crimes he'd been involved in.

"Don't you know it," he laughed. "You sticking around for dinner tonight?"

Since I'd promised her the night before that I would fix dinner, that wasn't what he was really asking. He wanted to know if Ty would be joining us. I didn't have the answer to that. I continued the conversation like this was any other day. "If she still keeps as close watch on my schedule as she used to, she'll know I'll be here. I might try to surprise you both with one of my new creations."

"Sounds good to me. She'll enjoy that." Mom instinctively knew what items would complement each other and enjoyed experimenting with different recipes. She had taught me to do the same. My recipes weren't always successful though. Tonight I would surprise her with one of my success stories that I'd tried for the potluck at work. All those on our floor had raved about it.

"Go introduce your friend to Skylar." He nodded his head towards the big barn-like structure. "Nice meeting you." He shook Ty's hand again. With a peck on my cheek, he watched as we walked away before he headed out to the vineyard. I could feel his eyes on my back. It wasn't hard to figure out where his thoughts were.

"Was there some unspoken message back there that I didn't understand?" Ty whispered as we walked towards the winery. "Do you suppose I met with his approval?"

"I think you passed inspection just fine," I laughed, poking him in the ribs with my elbow. "Skylar won't be as hard on you. Unless you try to steal her secrets on making wine, that is. She doesn't even share those with me."

"I promise I won't even try. I've made beer at home. If making wine is as long a process, I'd rather drink it than make it."

We stopped outside the big doors leading to the inner workings of the winery without going in. "Hey, Sky, do you mind if I bring someone in?" This was her territory. She didn't have many secrets to steal, but I wouldn't bring a stranger in without permission.

Involved in her work, she gave a startled jump, then turned to me. "Well, hi there." She came over to us with her hand outstretched. There was a big smile on her face. It wasn't hard for me guess what she was thinking.

Introducing them, I explained how I knew him to clear the path for her to invite him in. I didn't mention running out of gas. That would come later. "Glad you could come today." She led the way into the inner workings of the winery.

"Thanks for the tour, Skylar," Ty said when she was finished with the quick tour. "I really enjoyed it, but I'd better let you get back to work." He glanced at his watch. "It's almost time for you to open, and I need to get back to town." He turned to me. "If you have any more trouble, give me a call." There was a double meaning behind his words that I hoped Skylar didn't pick up on.

She lifted her eyebrows, but she didn't pursue the subject. I knew she would question me later though. "If you don't have plans for tonight," Sky said before he headed to his truck, "why don't you come back about six and stay for dinner. I know Greg and Dora would enjoy meeting you." Great, I groaned inwardly. Double the third degree. Poor Ty, I hoped he would survive, if he even agreed to it.

His gaze shifted to me. "If you don't mind, that sounds

great." He waited for me to nod.

"You don't have to subject yourself to dinner with the family, if you don't want to," I whispered as I walked to his truck with him.

"I don't mind if you don't." Okay, so this might not be as awkward as I feared. He leaned down, placing a kiss on my cheek before stepping up into the tall pickup. I watched as he drove off, feeling all warm and happy inside.

Once we were alone, she smiled at me. "He seems nice. Is he the reason you were late?" There was a teasing smile on her face. Everyone had been doing some matchmaking lately. "What was the trouble he mentioned?"

"Minor car trouble, no big deal," I shrugged. "Did you talk to the other owners last night?" I hoped the change of subject would take her mind off the reason for my tardiness.

She nodded her head. "That lawyer only showed up at a couple of other places." Worry clouded her features.

"What did Greg say?" We headed for the tasting room. Because of the quick tour she'd given Ty, we were running behind. If she didn't have things ready for the day, we needed to get busy.

"He's going to check out the lawyer. There isn't much else he can do for now. It isn't against the law to try to buy a business, even one that's not for sale." That depended on the method used. Someone had tried to sell her winery without her knowledge the year before. Because the realtor messed up, and put a for-sale sign along the highway, she had discovered it before any damage had been done.

Cody met us at the door. He was ready for a day of tourists. He lapped up the attention most people lavished on him.

By the end of the day, three more winery owners had called to say Mr. Earnhardt had been to visit them. Being forewarned of his possible visit, no one was willing to listen to his offer. Whoever his client was had picked a difficult task. Why not start your own winery instead of trying to buy one that was already up and running? You don't sell a profitable business.

There was another wrinkle though. Mr. Earnhardt wasn't the only one making offers to the different owners. A realtor had stopped at several wineries as well. The owners of the newest vineyard had jumped at the offer. Something was definitely going on. How had life gotten so complicated?

~~~

Ty followed Mom's car down the lane to the house that evening. I was waiting for him, hoping to ease the situation with an introduction. Instead of driving around to the back of the house as she usually did, she stopped out front.

"Hi, sweetie, how are you tonight?" Her question was for me, but she glanced back at Ty as he got out of his truck. "Do you know this young man?" There was a hopeful note in her voice.

"Yes, Mom, he's a friend." I laughed. In the small community, there aren't a lot of eligible men. She was always worried that I would meet someone who would whisk me away to other parts of the state, or country. I just hoped she wouldn't be too obvious, and scare him off. I turned to Ty as he joined us on the front porch.

"Ty, this is my Mom, Dora Barnes. Mom, this is Ty Fisher. He's one of the county paramedics." I didn't explain how he came to be here this morning. Greg was going to give him the third degree; I could only hope Mom didn't jump in with questions as well.

"It's nice to meet you, Ty. Will you be joining us for dinner tonight?"

"It's nice meeting you, Mrs. Barnes. Skylar invited me this morning when I stopped over with Pattiann. I hope that isn't going to be an inconvenience."

"Of course not. Any friend of Pattiann's is welcome, and none of this Mr. and Mrs. Stuff. We're just plain Joe and Dora." She turned towards the house, giving me a wink. I took that as a good sign. She had never been judgmental about any
~~~

of the men I dated. As long as they treated me with respect, she was fine. It was Greg who had objected to some of the boys and men I had chosen.

We were sitting on the front porch in front of Mom and Joe's side of the large house when Greg pulled into the lane. My stomach did a little flip. He had always put on a gruff big brother act when I brought a boyfriend home. I hoped he would behave himself now. "Ty? What are you doing here? Did something happen? I didn't get any calls from dispatch."

"Why would you assume I'm here to see you?" he said with a chuckle. "Can't a guy show up without people wondering why?" He stood up, holding out his hand to Greg. "How you doing?"

"You know each other?" I asked in surprise, before realizing it was a silly question. The sheriff's department and the fire department shared a building. Both men ignored me, so it didn't matter.

Greg accepted his handshake, but he still looked confused about Ty's presence here "I haven't seen you around much lately. I thought maybe you were busy with the Reserves."

"I've been busy, but not with the Reserves. The flu epidemic is keeping everyone hopping. What's your excuse? I haven't seen much of you lately either." Hopefully this exchange was simply friendly banter between two men. I wasn't always sure. Men communicated so differently from women.

"Well, I've been kind of busy myself," Greg said. "It might be a small county relatively free of crime, but I still have a lot of territory to cover." His sharp gaze kept moving between me and Ty. By now he had guessed Ty was here to see me, not him.

"Yeah, I guess, but that doesn't explain why you never told me you have a sister."

Uh oh, nothing good was going to come from that comment. "I don't go around announcing to every single man I meet that I have a little sister." I bristled at the 'little sister' comment, but didn't get a chance to complain. "I'm not in the matchmaking business. How do you know Pattiann?"

"You can stop right there, Greg," I stepped between the two men, hopefully putting an end to Greg's big brother act. I didn't need him running interference for me.

"I take it you two know each other." He frowned at me.

"Yes, we know each other," Ty said. "Do you have a problem with that?" He was confused.

"Enough of this nonsense." Mom had listened quietly until now. "I want all of you to stop right now. Pattiann, you need to go check on dinner. Greg, you've known Ty for several months, and I know you think he is a standup guy. So knock it off."

"But he's dating Pattiann," Greg objected. "That puts a whole different spin on things."

"How so?" Ty asked. "I'm still the same guy."

"We aren't exactly dating," I interrupted, stopping Greg from saying something we all might regret. "He helped me this morning when I had a little car trouble."

"What kind of car trouble? Why didn't you call me?"

I sighed, but before I could say anything Ty spoke up. "Well, I was kind of hoping this would count as a first date." He looked down at me before turning back to Greg. "Do you have a problem with that?" It was issued as sort of a challenge. One eyebrow lifted in question.

Before Greg could answer, Skylar called to him. "Honey, I need to see you for a minute." I'd been so busy trying to keep things from boiling over between the two men that I hadn't been aware she had gone back inside until right then.

"Be there in a minute." It looked like he couldn't make up his mind if he still wanted to argue with Ty.

"Now, dear." There was a touch of steel in her tone.

"I'll be right back. We aren't finished here."

"Yes, you are." Mom and I spoke at the same time.

There was a lot of whispering coming from inside, but we couldn't hear what they were saying. That was okay by me.

Skylar was as strong-minded as Greg. That meant they butted heads at times. I didn't want to be the cause of trouble between them, but I wouldn't let Greg choose who I spent time with either.

While they were having their little discussion, the rest of us headed for the kitchen. If I didn't want my experimental dinner ruined, I needed to keep a closer watch on it.

"If my being here is going to cause trouble, I'll leave." Ty was uncertain about what had just happened.

"That won't be necessary." Greg and Skylar stepped through the connecting door from the tasting room into Mom's kitchen. Greg looked only slightly embarrassed about his behavior. "I got a little carried away there for a minute," he said as a way of apology.

"You think?" I glared at him.

"I've been checking out your boyfriends for a long time, and some habits are hard to break. You'll always be my little sister."

"*Sister* being the operative word here, not *little*," I said with more than a little heat in my voice. "It's not your place to say who I can go out with. I'm not a child."

Greg and I didn't argue often, but when we did it could get pretty heated. Joe wasn't going to let that happen. "I think your mother said that was enough from both of you." Joe wasn't a big talker, but when he did speak, people listened. It was time for us to listen.

Greg drew in a deep breath, letting it out slowly. "Sorry, man." He held out his hand to Ty. "No hard feelings, okay?"

I waited to see what Ty would do. When he clasped Greg's hand, I released the breath I'd been holding. "I guess I can understand that. I never had a little sister, but I did have a big sister. There were a few guys she went out with that I wanted to punch, but they were all bigger than me at the time."

I was grateful that problem was all but forgotten. I really liked Ty, and I didn't want Greg to screw it up.

~~~
~~~

"What do you mean no one would listen to the offer?" he growled into the phone. "Did you even tell them what was being offered?" He could hear the other man gulp on the other end of the line.

"Apparently she warned the other owners that I would be stopping by. As long as their operation is profitable, they aren't interested in selling."

"Everything has a price" he sneered. "You just aren't offering them the right incentive."

"I don't think that's going to work with these folks. They all seem committed to what they're doing."

That wasn't the answer he wanted. "If you aren't willing to do what's necessary to accomplish what I want done, someone else will be."

The lawyer swallowed the lump in his throat. What he had to say next wasn't going to go over very well. "That small place you weren't interested in..." he paused, afraid of the reaction. "It's been sold. You aren't the only one interested in buying up some vineyards." He dreaded giving this sort of news, but it was better to get it over with sooner rather than later.

"What the hell?" The explosion that followed about blew out his ear drum. "Find out who bought it and make sure they change their mind." He slammed down the phone hard enough to break it. If someone was trying to mess things up for him, they would find out they were messing with the wrong person.

CHAPTER SIX

We spent most of dinner discussing the latest development with the vineyard owners. As usual, Sky and Greg had joined us in Mom and Joe's kitchen. "I can't believe Judy and her sister were so eager to sell," Mom said. "I thought it was a long-held dream of theirs to own a winery." After cleaning up from dinner, we sat on the wide porch enjoying the cool night air to continue the discussion.

Skylar nodded. "I think they got in a little over their heads. They didn't have enough capital to sustain them until the vines started producing." Some people make the mistake of thinking they can begin making wine from the first fruits of the vines. They end up with bad fruit and weak plants. You can't get good wine from bad plants.

"Have you talked to them? Do you know what their plans are now?" I asked.

Sky nodded again. "They haven't made up their minds. They made a good profit on their property, giving them some much-needed capital. If they decide to start over, they'll have the money to buy their grapes from another vineyard while they let their own vines mature."

"Did they say who purchased their place?" Greg joined the conversation. I knew what he was thinking. This whole deal seemed a little odd.

She shook her head, her blond hair falling over her shoulder. "That's the funny thing; it's supposed to remain confidential until everything is finalized. Whether it's the realtor or the lawyer, neither one is willing to give their buyer's name."

A realtor had stopped by earlier in the day making the same proposition as Mr. Earnhardt. He wasn't as pushy or as slippery, which was an improvement over the lawyer. Neither one would tell who was trying to buy the vineyards. If it was a legitimate business deal, why all the secrecy?

"Do you think they have the same client?"

As the sky darkened, I grew nervous. I wanted to leave before it was completely dark, but I also wanted to stay. I hadn't had a chance to talk to Mom about the situation at work either. I didn't want to say anything in front of Greg. He would be all for arresting Shirley. But as long as Rob was afraid to file a complaint, that wouldn't work. How many other men had she pulled this stunt on? I wondered.

Cody was dozing at Skylar's feet. He'd had a busy day greeting all of our visitors. It would be even busier the next two days, so he needed his rest. Suddenly he lifted his big head, giving a warning bark.

"What's wrong, boy?" Greg and Joe stood up, looking out at the vineyard. There was nothing to see in the growing darkness. Cody lay back down, but he kept his head up, scanning the dark vineyard.

That was my cue to go home. I'd put it off long enough. "I'd better head home." There was no enthusiasm in my voice. There would be very little traffic until I got closer to town. I should be able to tell if someone was following me. I had my cell phone handy if that happened. I wouldn't hesitate calling Greg then, no matter what the consequences were. Someone had been in my house. I was certain of that. Maybe I should have told him, but it was too late for that now.

I continued to hesitate long enough that Mom frowned at me. "Are you all right, Honey? Is something bothering you?"

Lost in my thoughts, I gave a start. "No, of course not. Just daydreaming I guess." I didn't like hiding this from her, but the alternative wasn't very appealing. Greg would have a deputy patrol past my house, or he'd insist I move out here with them. I wasn't going to allow either option.

"Maybe tomorrow we'll have more time to visit," I said to change the subject. Saturdays were always busy with tourists, especially on festival weekends. Sky was the only winemaker in the area to make fruit wines and mead. She was getting a pretty good following, and had won several awards for them.

People were always interested in trying what she had.

Placing a kiss on Mom's cheek before she asked any more questions, I moved down the steps to my car. Ty offered to follow me home. He was still worried about my gas situation I guess. I was grateful he had refrained from mentioning it to Greg. After the way he'd reacted to Ty's presence, Ty could guess how Greg would react to someone syphoning gas from my car.

The headlights in my rearview mirror from Ty's big truck were comforting. I still wasn't sure whether I'd been followed from the diner. If someone thought about following me now, Ty's presence would deter them. I hoped.

Driving past Templeton Vineyards, I could see Chase sitting outside. It had to be a lonesome existence for him without any family and only a few friends. The winery owners were a close-knit group, but most had families here. Chase had been so intent on making a go of his winery when he moved here that he had neglected his social life. Now, when he should be enjoying his success, he had no one to share it with.

Bonnie's pretty face popped into my mind. She was looking for some excitement. I didn't think Chase qualified as exciting, but maybe they could be friends. I didn't want to play matchmaker, but it wouldn't hurt to introduce them, and see what came of it.

I'd mentioned that I had a friend looking for something to do on her days off. Maybe working for Chase would be a good fit for both of them. I decided to put some thought into that later.

Ty pulled to the side of the road in front of my house when I pulled into my driveway. All the way into town I had debated whether to invite him in. It was a little early in our relationship for something like that though. Besides, I had a visitor waiting for me. The strong beam from the yard light illuminated even the far corners of my small yard, including Bonnie. She was sitting on my front porch looking lost and forlorn.

"Is everything okay?" Ty called to me. I wasn't sure if he knew who my visitor was. She stood up, giving him a wave.

"Yes, it's fine. I think," I whispered to myself. Giving him another wave, I turned to her. "Are you all right? What are you doing out here?"

She lifted her shoulders, letting them drop in a dejected shrug. "I came over to see if you wanted to do something tonight. It's Friday. Shouldn't we be out partying? Did I interrupt something?" She looked at Ty who was waiting for us to go inside. Her cheeks had turned a pretty pink.

"No, of course not," I said with a laugh. "Come on in. Maybe we can think of something fun to do that doesn't include going to a bar." I waved at Ty. "Thanks for following me home. I'll see you later."

Unlocking the door, I slipped my hand around the door post to flip on the light without going inside. I pushed the door open, surveying the room. Nothing was out of place in the living room and kitchen. Unless someone was hiding behind the breakfast bar, I silently qualified.

"Is something wrong?" Ty called out again. I could see the worried frown on his face.

"No, everything's okay." My voice squeaked slightly. I waved again.

"Are we going in or just stand out here looking inside?" Bonnie didn't understand why I was hesitating.

Releasing the breath I'd been holding, I gave a nervous laugh. "Sorry. Of course we're going in." I went in ahead of her. If someone was waiting to attack me, I didn't want her to get hurt in my place.

Everything was as I'd left it that morning. My Louisville Slugger was propped beside the door. I planned on getting a couple more so there was always one within reach.

"You live here, right?" Bonnie spoke up again.

Giving a startled squeal, I whirled around to face her. For a short minute while I surveyed the room again, I'd forgotten she was with me. "Okay, what's going on?" She frowned at me. "Why are you so spooked about going into your own home?"

I started to deny the accusation, but she held up her hand. "Don't bother denying it. Your face is as white as a sheet." Taking my arm, she led me over to the couch, sitting down beside me. "Spill it, girl." How could she be so insightful one minute and naïve the next?

Before answering, I stood up again. Going to the door that she'd left open, I closed and locked it. Flopping down beside her, I rested my head on the back of the couch. "You must think I'm some kind of a nut." She didn't say anything, waiting for me to continue. With a heavy sigh, I did just that. It took several minutes to tell her what had me so spooked.

"Now do you see why I didn't want you going to the bar alone?" I asked once I finished. "If someone followed me from the diner, what would happen at a bar?"

"What did your brother say? He's the sheriff, right?"

"Um, well, I didn't say anything to him."

"Why not? If someone was following you and was in your house, you need to tell him." She looked around the small living room like she expected someone to jump out of the closet.

"You don't understand," I started to say.

"I understand all right. You don't want your brother to get all overprotective. But isn't that his job as a big brother?" She gave a wistful sigh. "I always wished I had a big brother or sister. Besides," her voice gained strength again, "this could be serious. You thought I was being reckless even thinking about going to a bar alone. What do you call this?"

I huffed out a breath. "I know you're right, but I know how he can be with things like this. He still treats me like I'm fifteen. Or five," I added. "There is nothing Greg's department can do. Nothing was taken, and there was no sign of forced entry." I tried to explain so it didn't sound like I was being careless.

"Knowing someone can get in your house, aren't you

afraid to stay here alone?" An involuntary shiver shook her body.

I gulped, but put on a brave face. "This is my home. I'm not going to let anyone run me off."

"Uh huh, is that what the baseball bat is for?" She tilted her head to one side, giving me a grin. "What's with that chair under the door knob? I saw that trick in an old movie once. Will it really keep someone from getting in?"

"I'm not sure if it will keep anyone out," I laughed with her. "But they'll have to work a little harder, and make a lot of noise in the process. If anyone does get in, I can fend them off with my trusty bat until the police get here. In fact, I plan on getting a couple more."

She laughed, but gave another shiver. "I'd never be able to hit anything. My folks didn't let me play sports in school."

"I played on the high school and college softball teams," I said. "I wasn't half bad either. At least I'll be able to hit what I'm aiming for. I will defend myself. No one is going to turn me into a victim." I was thinking of Rob. Because he wouldn't do anything to stop her, he was allowing Shirley to do just that. If someone was following me, or breaking into my home, I wasn't going to roll over and play dead.

"I don't like living alone," she said in a small voice. "Until I moved here I'd always lived with my parents. So far, I haven't found anyone that wants to split the rent. My apartment is too small for two people anyway." I'd opened one of my favorite wines, and she stared into the glass like she could find a roommate there.

A thought came to me like a light bulb going off in my head. "Would you like to move in with me?" The words were out of my mouth before I could even think about them.

Her face was filled with shock and excitement. "Are you serious? You'd be willing to let me move in with you?" She made it sound like a miracle had just happened.

She held her breath while I thought about my suggestion. I nodded my head. "Yeah, I don't see why not. We get along great. Unless you're some kind of serial killer, or maybe a real slob, that is." I cocked my head to one side, teasing her.

She shook her head no to both questions, like she thought I was serious. "My parents would have skinned me alive if I left things lying around." She released a heavy sigh. "I always told myself when I had my own place I would do anything I wanted. But it turns out my parents are still in my head. When I drop my clothes on the floor, I can hear my mom telling me to pick them up. Pathetic, right?"

I laughed and shook my head. "Not really. I know what you mean though. I think that's what parents are supposed to do to keep their kids in line even after they're grown up." I drew a deep breath. "So, do you want to move in here? After what I just told you, you wouldn't be afraid?" I held up my glass like I was offering a toast.

"Two are better than one." She touched her glass to mine with a soft clink. "Thank you so much." She pulled me in for a quick hug. "I really do hate living alone. That's why I never want to go home after work." She whispered the last.

"Me, too." I giggled. We'd finished off one bottle and started on another one. I'd never had more than two glasses at one time, and we were both beginning to feel the effects of that much wine.

"You were right. Your sister-in-law makes good wine. The only wine I've had before is sour." Bonnie held up her nearly empty glass, looking at the amber liquid. "So how can I get a job in one of the tasting rooms? It sounds like it would be fun. It's better than sitting at home alone on my four days off." I'd been telling her about working there on the weekends for several weeks.

"I'll call Skylar, and ask if she needs any help tomorrow. If she doesn't, there is someone else I can call." I figured I could call Chase, since he had suggested I come to work for him. He'd probably been joking. Then again, maybe not.

Sky answered her phone on the third ring. "What's the matter? Did you chase Ty off already?" She teased.

"I figured Greg would come after him with a hatchet if he stuck around very long. It's a little early in our relationship for that. Besides, someone was sitting on my porch when I got home."

"Oh my gosh, why didn't you call Greg? Are you all right? Should I send him over?"

I laughed. "No need. I'm fine. My friend from the hospital was waiting for me to get home."

Sky gave a sigh of relief, telling Greg to relax, I was fine. "You had me going for a minute. What can I do for you?"

Before explaining the reason for my call, I looked at the clock. "I'm sorry for calling so late. I didn't realize what time it was. I hope I didn't interrupt something…important?" My voice rose at the end, turning my statement into a question.

"If you were interrupting something, I wouldn't have answered the phone," she joked back. "So what can I do for you?"

After explaining that Bonnie wanted to help out in the tasting room, she was quick to agree. "If you want to bring her along, that's fine with me. Betsy will be here. She can show Bonnie the ropes."

I debated my next move, deciding it would be best to start her at Sky's tasting room before introducing her to Chase. I wanted to run that by Sky in person first. I didn't think she'd object, but I wanted to be sure. "Okay, we'll be there before you open up. Have fun tonight." I could hear her laughter as I hung up.

"Well, it's settled." I turned back to Bonnie. "You can go out with me tomorrow, and get a feel for what we do. It isn't rocket science, so you'll catch on fast. I know of someone else who is looking for help in his tasting room."

"Him?" Her eyes lit up. "Someone you'd like to tell me about?"

"Sure, why not." I paused, drawing a big breath. I knew what she was thinking, but she was wrong. Chase was an acquaintance, or maybe a friend, I decided. He'd never confided in Skylar about his family history. I guess that made us more than simple acquaintances.

"He sounds interesting," Bonnie said when I gave her a brief history of Skylar's relationship with Chase. I didn't repeat what he'd told me at the diner. It was up to him to tell people about his family problems, not me. "A single man younger than forty definitely sounds interesting." I noticed that she'd upped the age on the single men in town.

"You want to tell me why Ty was with you? Are you sure I didn't interrupt something?"

"I invited him to have dinner at my mom's place tonight. He followed me home to make sure I was okay." I'd already told her about the empty gas tank.

She stood up, swaying slightly. "Wow, who knew you could get tipsy on two glasses of wine?" She steadied herself on the arm of the couch.

"Two glasses?" I pointed at the two bottles. We'd finished the second one by that time. "I think you'd better sit down." She gladly obliged, resting her head against the back of the couch. "You'd better stay here tonight. We're about the same size. You can wear something of mine tomorrow."

Without a word of argument, she followed me to the spare bedroom. She could sleep on the daybed in there. We got the bed made, and I handed her an oversized tee shirt to sleep in. She splashed water on her face then fell on top of the covers. "We'll find you something to wear in the morning," I said as I turned out the light. I don't think she even heard me. Her eyes were already closed when I walked out of the room.

~~~

This wasn't as easy as he expected. Money usually talked louder than dreams. He'd already been in this godforsaken town longer than he wanted. Someone else was trying to buy up the wineries. He didn't like competition. When he set his mind to something, he didn't let anything or anyone get in his way.

Getting that stupid boy to come to his senses wasn't going
~~~

to be easy. He was as stubborn as the day was long. But that didn't matter. Nothing was going to stop him from accomplishing what he set out to do.

In hindsight, he could see where he'd gone wrong. Telling him he couldn't do something had never worked. Buying up the various wineries around his operation might help to convince him he was serious. Expansion was the root of any big company. Expanding into the wine business made sense. He could see that now. Convincing that stubborn boy to join forces was going to take some doing, but it was time for that boy to start toeing the line.

CHAPTER SEVEN

"I thought the ER was crazy," Bonnie whispered. The tasting room had only been open two hours, but people were standing three deep waiting for their turn at the tasting bar. "No wonder bartenders love their jobs. This is so much fun!" I wasn't sure if she meant selling the wine or flirting with single men. She did both very well.

"Aren't you glad you came?" I whispered back. She gave a quick nod. That was all the time we had for any chit chat between customers. As one group left, another took their place at the tasting bar. Betsy and I were working as quickly as possible without being rude, but we still couldn't keep up with the crowd.

Skylar still enjoyed interacting with the customers, and spent time visiting with return customers and greeting new ones. Bonnie had caught on quickly and was a big help. We were glad to have her to take up the slack. On normal weekends, it wasn't necessary to have more than two or three working, but festival weekends could get exceptionally busy.

Skylar had recently enlarged the tasting room, and added several bistro tables and chairs along with a loveseat where people could sit and enjoy a full glass of wine. She also offered cheese and meat platters customers could order. That helped cut down on people drinking on an empty stomach. All of the winery owners offered designated drivers a free bottle of water or soda to cut down on drunk driving as well.

There hadn't been time to ask her if it was all right for me to introduced Bonnie to Chase. I didn't see any reason for her to object though. I'd check with him later to see if he needed help at his place.

I gathered from what he'd said at the café that he didn't have help in the tasting room on a regular basis. On a particularly busy weekend, he would be stretched to the limit. Maybe Bonnie would be the right fit, and it would benefit both of them. Whether he wanted to admit it or not, he was still trying to prove himself to his father, even if the man never came to see what he had accomplished.

It was close to closing time when Ty came in. With him were three good-looking men. Each one would qualify for a spot on the firemen's annual calendar. Bonnie and I both forgot about being tired, and stood a little straighter. Ty's bright green eyes settled on me from the back of the room, a smile teasing the corners of his mouth.

"Wow," Bonnie breathed out a sigh. "Four hunky guys in one place, it's almost too good to be true." She was going to start drooling at any minute.

While they waited for their turn at the bar, Ty's gaze never left me. I could feel my face heating up, but there was nothing I could do about it.

"I don't think he's here for wine tasting," Sky whispered, bringing my errant thoughts back on track.

"I don't know what you're talking about."

"Um hmmm," was her only comment. Her giggle caused my face to get even hotter.

As the room began to clear out, Ty's group stepped up to the bar. He gave me a dazzling smile while the others zeroed in on Bonnie. I didn't think she'd mind at all. She was having the time of her life fielding all the flirtatious remarks with ones of her own. She was a born flirt in spite of the sheltered life she'd led until now. Her newfound freedom had gone to her head. I just hoped she wouldn't let it go too far.

"I enjoyed the wine you served last night," Ty said. "I thought I'd come out and give the rest of Skylar's selection a try." A teasing smile tickled the corners of his lips.

"Oh, um, sure," I stammered. We'd spent several hours together the night before, so why was I suddenly tongue-tied? Enjoying my dilemma, Sky took over, sliding the wine list in front of him.

"It's good to see you again, Ty." She reached across the bar to shake his hand. "Here's our wine selection." A teasing smile lit up her face. "Do you prefer red or white, sweet or dry?" It was pretty much her standard line when people came in for the first time.

It was several seconds before Ty shifted his gaze to her. With a sheepish grin, he looked down at the list. "Um, I guess I prefer white, semi-sweet."

I poked her with my elbow. "I've got this. Go help someone else," I whispered. Her laughter trailed back to me as she walked away.

He paused for a moment before going on. "I know it's rather short notice, but if you don't have any plans tonight would you like to join me for dinner?"

My heart gave a funny flutter. I didn't want to appear overly eager. But I didn't want him to think I wasn't interested either. "I don't have plans, and I'd love to have dinner with you."

"That's a great idea." One of Ty's friends had been eavesdropping and spoke up. The room was empty except for the four firemen, Skylar, Bonnie and me. After most of the crowd left, Betsy had gone home for the day. "But we're short two women." He gave Skylar a wink. "What about you? Are you available to join us? Then we'd only be short one."

Holding up her left hand to show off her wedding ring, she laughed. "I'm not sure my husband would approve. Unless you're inviting him along?" She lifted one eyebrow.

He shrugged, laughing with her. "Sure bring him along. The more the merrier. You got any single friends besides these two?"

She shook her head, her blonde ponytail flopping over her shoulder. "Sorry, you'll have to find your own dates. I'm no longer in the matchmaking business." Her last remark was meant for me. I was hoping no one else caught her drift. Coming out from behind the bar, she went over to the door. "It doesn't look like anyone else is going to be stopping in, so I'm going to lock up. Take your time finishing your tastings."

It was decided that we'd go out as a group, without pairing

off. That made the evening more informal, and we didn't have to dress up. Bonnie could shower at my place, and wear one of my blouses with her jeans. She could spend the night with me again. This was the excitement she'd been looking for.

"We'll pick you up at your place," Ty said as they got ready to leave. "How does six o'clock sound?"

"Great," I gave him a smile. My heart was thumping so loudly I thought he could probably hear it. It wasn't exactly the date I'd been hoping for, but it was a start.

Driving past Templeton Vineyards on our way back to town, I slowed down. "I'm going to check with Chase to see if he needs help tomorrow," I said, pointing at the dark house. At this time of night I was surprised that he wasn't sitting on the porch. There was a light on in his winery and the big doors were open. He was probably working late, I told myself. I dismissed him from my thoughts. We were in a hurry to get ready before the guys came to pick us up.

Driving past The Lamplighter, I slowed to a crawl. "Aren't you glad you didn't go there?" The parking lot was full, and people were heading inside. My mouth dropped open when I spotted a familiar figure. "What's he doing here?" I muttered.

"Who? Who are you talking about?" Bonnie stared out the window, but she didn't recognize anyone.

"Um, it's nobody. I must have been mistaken." I started having second thoughts about introducing Bonnie to Chase. He didn't strike me as the type to appreciate the seedy bar scene so what was he doing here?

The light had been on in his winery, and the door was open. I had assumed he was still working. Since he was in town, why were the doors open? I hoped he had security guys to make sure nothing was stolen. After my experience a couple of nights ago, I wondered if a burglary ring was targeting New Haven. Four-legged vandals would also cause a lot of damage if they went in looking for something to eat. I'd figure out what to do about Chase later. Giving a mental shake, I pulled back onto the road. It was time to get ready for our date.

~~~

"This has been the best day of my life." Bonnie flopped down on the couch. It was after one in the morning. In a few short hours we would be getting up for church. Neither of us was ready to go to bed though.

"I've never had so much fun on what turned out to be a non-date." She laughed. Growing serious, she turned to me. "You didn't mind that we messed up your date with Ty, did you?"

"No, this was fun."

"But it wasn't really a date for you." She continued to worry I was upset with her.

"It wasn't the strict definition of a date, but it was still fun. It also took away the first date jitters." After leaving the restaurant, Walt, one of Ty's friends, had suggested we go dancing. An old abandoned building had been turned into a night club of sorts several years ago. They served drinks and finger foods, and it was classier than The Lamplighter. The bouncer didn't tolerate drunks, and showed them to the door at the first signs of trouble.

"I told you there were nice single men in town. You didn't even have to go to a bar to find one, or three," I added on a laugh. She stood up to do a little dance. She was still full of energy from the fun she'd had.

"We'd better get some sleep now," I suggested. My energy had started to desert me. "We have another full day tomorrow. Next week I'll introduce to one of the other winemakers." If it had Chase been going into The Lamplighter, it wouldn't have done any good to call when we first got home. I decided to wait and call him during the week.

~~~

"What did you find out today?" He snarled into the phone. He was getting impatient. It was time to get this business done.

"No one knows who the other buyer is."

"Or they're not saying. You need to get this straightened out. I don't want any more excuses."

"No one wants to sell a profitable business, not even for a bigger profit," he argued. "These people are pretty committed to what they're doing. You should know that. As long as you want to expand, why not just buy some of the vacant land that's for sale?" He'd asked that question before.

"My reasons are just that, mine. Stop asking questions and get this done, or I'll find someone willing to do business my way. Do I make myself clear?"

"Yes sir." As usual, the caller didn't hear his response. He had already disconnected. If he isn't going to listen to me, why bother asking questions, he thought. He released a heavy sigh. There was something squirrely about that guy. Why not just go talk to these people himself? After all, he knows them, right? "Not that I mind the money he's paying me," he muttered. "Mine is not to reason why, mine is just to do as I'm told." He misquoted the famous saying by Alfred Lord Tennyson.

~~~

The flu epidemic was still going on when we returned to work, but there was a light at the end of the tunnel. Fewer patients were being brought in by ambulance. That was a good thing, but that meant fewer chances to see Ty. It also meant there was more time for Shirley to pressure Rob into giving in to her demands.

I was still hoping he would report her actions to HR. I hadn't had time to ask Mom's opinion about what I'd overheard, but I was certain what she would say. I didn't want to get Rob in trouble with his girlfriend, but letting Shirley get away with what she was doing made me guilty as well.

If someone didn't report her, she would keep doing this to others. How many others had she threatened if they didn't comply with her wishes? Why didn't anyone complain? Was it like Rob said, that no one would believe they were being threatened? Or were they too embarrassed to tell?

When an ambulance pulled into the bay, my heart skipped a beat as Ty stepped out pulling a gurney out with him. He hadn't come out to Sky Vineyards on Sunday, but I couldn't
~~~

expect him to spend his days off at the winery while I worked. We'd only had one date, or semi-date, I reminded myself.

"She's in pretty bad shape," he stated as he pushed the gurney through the doors. The woman was on oxygen, and they had run an IV line. I started to follow him to an exam room.

"I'll take this one." Shirley almost pushed me out of the way. This was the second time she'd taken over a case when Ty was the paramedic on duty.

Raising his eyebrows, Ty looked at me, but he didn't comment. There wasn't time for anything else to be said as she pulled the curtain closed behind them. The paramedics didn't normally remain in the exam room after giving their report on the patient's condition. Was Shirley branching out with her sexual harassment, and including the paramedics?

What would he do if she propositioned him the way she had Rob? She couldn't threaten his job since he didn't work for the hospital.

"Where's Ty?" Angelo stopped beside me with an armload of supplies for the ambulance.

"He's helping out with the patient." I nodded at the closed curtain.

"Again?" He chuckled. "Say a prayer that he's got stronger resolve than some." Giving his head a shake, he headed outside with his supplies.

Once again, I thought that meant he knew all about Shirley's activities. If she had been harassing some of the paramedics, why hadn't someone reported her?

"Thank you for assisting me in there, Ty." Shirley smiled up at him. "I don't know what we'd do without you, um, the paramedics." She gave his arm a pat. "We're shorthanded because of the large number of patients, but we know we can count on you to assist us." She fluttered her eyelashes at him.

"Glad I could help." He nodded his head, stepping back from her. "See you around." Walking past the desk, he gave me a wink. "See you ladies later."

When another ambulance pulled into the bay an hour later, Shirley was right there to greet the paramedics. She was all business, but I noticed she had put on lipstick and fluffed up her long chestnut hair.

The only female paramedic with the county fire department pulled the gurney out of the ambulance. If anyone could make me green with envy, it was Wanda. At five seven, she had an hour glass figure. Her black hair shone almost blue in the sunlight. Today she wore it pulled back in a messy ponytail. On me it would look like a rat's nest, but on Wanda it was oddly stylish. Somehow she even managed to make the heavy uniforms of the fire department look elegant.

"Hey, Shirley," Wanda smiled, not noticing, or ignoring the disappointment on the other woman's face. "Little Billy here fell out of a tree in his backyard. He's got a big bump on his head and a broken leg. I told him you were going to fix him right up with a neat cast for all his friends to sign. He's really being brave and said he didn't need his mom. I told him she'd feel better if she came to check on him."

She kept up a cheerful line of chatter as they wheeled the gurney into the exam room. Billy was all of five or six years old, with tearful blue eyes. He was trying to live up to her announcement of how brave he was. Wanda didn't give Shirley a chance to pass Billy off on someone else. Shirley didn't keep her in the exam room the way she had with Ty either. Now that I knew what she was doing, it was extremely obvious. I wondered how I had missed it before.

Bonnie was almost jumping out of her skin when I walked up to the nurses' station a few minutes later. A big vase of flowers was sitting on the counter. "These are for you. Hurry up and open the card," she gushed. "Maybe Ty sent them."

The card simply said "Thanks" and was signed with a "C."

"Who's C?" she asked, reading the card over my shoulder. "What's he thanking you for?"

My first thought was of Chase, but why would he be sending me flowers? I'd enjoyed the time we spent at the diner, but it wasn't like it had been a date. I had no idea who else would be sending me flowers.

She nudged me to get my attention. "Who's C?" she asked again.

"I have no idea." She lifted one eyebrow, registering her doubt. "Really, I don't know who sent them."

"A secret admirer?" A big smile spread across her face. "That's so romantic."

"No. It's creepy." My mind raced over what happened this past weekend. Someone had followed me home from the diner, someone had been in my house while I was gone and syphoned the gas out of my car. Now I get a big vase of flowers. I didn't want her to change her mind about moving in with me. Maybe if I didn't live alone, whoever was doing this would leave me alone.

"Where did these come from?" Shirley leaned in to smell the different flowers a few minutes later. She sounded curious, not upset. Billy had been taken to X-Ray, freeing her up to come to the desk.

"Pattiann has a secret admirer," Bonnie answered for me.

"Really?" She looked at me with obvious suspicion. "Could they be from a certain paramedic?" She lifted one eyebrow.

"Not unless he changed his name." I didn't pretend not to know who she was talking about. "The card with signed with the initial C."

She brightened at that. "I don't know of any paramedics with that initial, not even the married ones." She gave a small laugh. "You might want to take them to the break room before they get knocked off the counter. It looks like we're in for another busy day." As long as they didn't come from one of the men she was interested in, she no longer cared who sent them.

I spent the rest of the afternoon trying to figure out who had sent the flowers, and why. If Chase sent them, why not sign his name instead of using an initial? There was something unsettling about the situation.

Leaving work, I made a last-minute decision and headed out of town. It was almost dark. If someone followed me, I wouldn't be able to see the driver or what they were driving. But I wanted to talk to Chase. I went over several scenarios how to begin asking if he sent the flowers. No matter how I phrased my question, it was going to sound like I was fishing for a compliment. Giving up, I decided to wing it. The truth usually worked best no matter what the question should be.

Chase was sitting on the porch in front of his house like he did on most evening when I left Sky Vineyards. A glass of wine was sitting at his elbow. A big smile spread across his face when I stepped out of my car. "This is a pleasant surprise. What brings you out this way?"

"Um, well," I stammered. "I wanted to ask you something."

"Okay, ask away." He offered me the chair he'd vacated when I pulled up. The fact that there was only one chair on the porch said a lot. He wasn't used to having company. "Can I offer you a glass of wine?" He sat down on the porch railing, facing me.

"No, thank you." I needed to keep a clear head. "Um, I was wondering if maybe, um." I was making a muddle of this. Finally I blurted it out. "Did you send me flowers today?"

"No, but now I wish I'd thought of it." A puzzled frown creased his forehead. "Why would you think I sent them?"

"Oh, um, someone sent them, but the card was only signed with a C." That sounded lame. His name wasn't the only one that began with C. I could feel my face growing hot. I hoped he didn't think this was a come-on of some kind.

"Like I said, I wish I'd thought of it. Your boyfriend's name doesn't begin with a C, does it?"

"Um, no." It was too soon to call Ty my boyfriend, but I didn't say that. Giving him the impression that I had a boyfriend seemed like a good idea at the moment.

"Maybe one of your patients sent them," he suggested.

"Yeah, that's probably it," I agreed. That was as good an answer as any other. Embarrassed now, I stood up. "I'd better head back to town. It's getting late."

"Not that late. Stay and have a glass with me." He lifted his wine glass. "I don't think you've ever tried my wines."

"I don't drink when I'm driving." That sounded rather of sanctimonious, and I attempted to clarify what I meant. "Even one glass of wine messes with my head enough that I shouldn't drive. I guess that makes me a real light-weight." My face felt like it was on fire by now. I needed to get out of there before I made a bigger mess of things.

But he laughed. "I guess it wouldn't look good for the sheriff's sister to be stopped for DUI either. Maybe some other time when you aren't driving you'll try one of my wines. I do make some pretty good wine, even if I do say so myself." A slick smile slid across his face.

This was the over-blown, self-assured man that Skylar and Joe always talked about. He might be reluctant to talk about himself, but his wine was another matter.

Making an excuse and a hasty retreat, I headed for my car. Whatever possessed me to go see him? I silently questioned my motives. It was just some stupid flowers. He probably thought I was interested in him, when that was the last thing I needed or wanted. He was a nice guy, but not the one for me. It was too early to say Ty was the special one, but I did have high hopes.

When headlights flashed in my rearview mirror nearly blinding me, I brought my thoughts back to the present. A big truck was riding my bumper. If I had to stop suddenly, he'd be in my trunk. All I could see were headlights, and a shiny grill in my mirror.

Glancing down at the speedometer, I realized my speed had slowed as my mind was occupied with the matter of the flowers. Speeding up, I hoped the driver would back off, but he stayed right with me. My heart was in my throat. I wanted to call Greg, but was afraid to take my eyes off the road long enough to reach for my phone.

As we got closer to town, the roar of the big truck's engine revved up as he finally passed me. The windows were tinted dark so I couldn't see the driver. Trucks were standard vehicles in and around New Haven. They all looked alike to me. Even Ty drove a truck.

So did Chase. The thought popped unbidden into my mind. I'd been lost in my thoughts when I left Templeton Vineyards, and hadn't noticed if Chase had followed me. But why would he? I didn't know what to think. If it had been Chase going into The Lamplighter the other night, maybe he was going there again.

CHAPTER EIGHT

"How are things, Rob?" I hoped my question wasn't so cryptic that he wouldn't know what I was asking, but no one else would figure it out.

A dark frown drew his brows together. "Everything is fine." Sarcasm dripped from his voice. "Forget you ever heard anything, and keep your mouth shut." My mouth dropped open in surprise at his harsh words. He acted like I'd done something wrong.

The day was almost over when Shirley came out of one of the empty rooms. She looked like the cat that ate the canary. Her steps faltered slightly when she noticed me, but she recovered quickly. With a curt nod, she continued down the hall. My feet felt rooted to the floor, and I couldn't have walked away if I wanted to. Unless she'd been alone, I had a pretty good idea what she'd been doing in the empty room.

When the door opened again, Rob stepped out. As Shirley had, he paused when he saw me. "Don't say a word, Pattiann." He got right in my face. "Not to anyone, or I swear you'll be sorry." He was threatening me? What had I done? He marched off without a backward glance.

"She is such a witch," Martha, one of the other nurses, came up beside me. "Does she really think we don't know what she's up to with every male under thirty? The administration is the only ones playing dumb. They should have hired from within instead of hiring her." She stomped off leaving me with my mouth hanging open again.

Finally managing to close my mouth, I wondered yet again if I had been the only one oblivious to what Shirley had been up to. How long had this been going on? What she was doing was wrong. If others were aware of what she was doing, why didn't someone say something? "See something, say something," didn't just pertain to terrorism. If you're aware of a crime, you should report it. So why was I keeping quiet? I told myself it was because Rob asked me to. But was that the real reason?

Bonnie followed me outside a short time later. I'd had it for the day, and couldn't wait to go home. "There's a new movie playing at the theater tonight," she said. "How about going with me? I heard it's supposed to be really good."

"What about getting a head start on packing?" We were both excited about her moving in with me. She only had a month left on her lease which gave us plenty of time to move her things. Mom had left most of the furniture we had shared when she and Joe got married. I still needed to decide what to keep in order to make room for Bonnie.

Bonnie looked sheepishly down at the ground. "I'm renting a furnished apartment, so I only have to pack my clothes and a few personal things," she finally admitted. "Until I graduated from college, I lived with my parents. That's part of the reason I took the job here. They would have expected me to continue living at home if I got a job in Peoria, or anywhere close by." She blew out a breath, ruffling her bangs.

"Please go with me," she pleaded. "It's just for a couple of hours. You'll be home before ten."

Since when couldn't I stay up past ten and still get up early the next morning? Her words made me feel as old as Methuselah. I needed to get out more. "All right, I'll go. Can we get something to eat first?" Like most days, lunch was just a distant memory.

"They have hot dogs, soft pretzels, popcorn, or anything else you can imagine at the snack bar. Let's go." She was excited and in a hurry. I wondered just how sheltered she had been. Didn't her parents even let her go to the movies?

I almost objected to buying anything from the snack bar. Theater prices were always inflated, but that would make me seem cheap as well as old. I nodded my head. "Okay, let's go."

The movie was better than I expected, and popcorn made a good meal. Not exactly nutritious, but it tasted good and filled the empty hole in my stomach. It was just before ten when we walked outside. We were still in our hospital scrubs, and the cool night air gave me a chill. I wrapped my arms around my waist, wishing I hadn't left my sweater in the car.

Ahead of us a familiar figure hurried through the parking lot. "Hi, Chase," I called out, but he didn't turn around.

"Chase who?" Bonnie was on high alert. "Is that the guy who sent you the flowers? His name begins with C."

Before I could draw his attention, he disappeared in the maze of cars and trucks. He probably didn't hear me, I reasoned. But he hadn't been that far away. It seemed like he'd stepped up his pace when I called to him. Why would he do that?

"Who's Chase?" Bonnie broke in on my rambling thoughts.

"Chase Templeton owns the winery next to Sky Vineyards. I guess it wasn't him." They say that everyone has a double somewhere in the world. It would be quite a coincidence for Chase's double to be right here in New Haven.

I shook off those thoughts. "Thanks for asking me tonight. It was fun. I haven't gone to a movie in a long time. Of course, there hasn't been much worth watching either." I was beginning to shiver. "I'll see you in the morning." Giving her a hug, I hurried to my car.

A big truck pulled out of the parking lot ahead of me. Trucks look pretty much alike, but this one looked a lot like the one Chase drives. A lot like the truck that rode my bumper the night before, I added silently. I couldn't tell if there was any writing on the side door panels advertising Templeton Vineyards.

It had been a foolish mistake to ask if he'd sent me flowers. I wasn't going to make the same mistake, and ask if he'd been at the movie tonight. I didn't want him to think I was interested in him, or worse, stalking him.

The truck headed out of town, and I followed along to see if it was going to Templeton Vineyards. When I missed my turn to go home I gave myself a mental shake. This was beyond ridiculous. I was becoming paranoid with all that had happened recently. If it was Chase, how would I explain following him? Besides, what difference did it make if he went to the movie?

I turned at the next corner, heading back to my house. I was tired, and I needed to get up for work in the morning.

~~~

It had been a long day, and he'd missed dinner again. It was time to get something to eat. Pulling into the parking lot of the one decent restaurant in town, he slammed on the brakes. What the hell is he doing here? He stared at the man crossing the lot.

Realization hit him like a hammer to the head. "He's the one trying to buy up the vineyards," he muttered. Slumping down in the seat, he covertly watched as the man made his way through the parking lot to his car.

He should have known that's who his competition was. Why the sudden interest in the wine industry?

Dinner would have to wait. When the big car pulled out of the parking lot, he followed along behind. The game just got more interesting. He needed to scout out the competition. He wasn't going to let anyone, especially that man, beat him at his own game.

~~~

It was business as usual for Shirley the following day. She acted like I hadn't almost caught her in a very compromising situation. She didn't seem too embarrassed by that fact either. Rob, on the other hand, was a nervous wreck. I wasn't quite sure what to say to him, so I avoided him. Had he really threatened me, or was he simply upset by what he had done? I wasn't sure what he thought he could do to me if I said anything. I felt sorry for his girlfriend though.

I was alone for a few minutes at the desk when Rob stopped beside me. "I'm sorry for the way I reacted yesterday," he whispered. "I hope you know I didn't mean what I said. I just need you to keep quiet about what happened."

"I'm not the only one that knows what's going on, Rob." His face blanched at my words. I knew he was afraid his girlfriend would find out. Why would she blame him? That would be like blaming a rape victim when she was raped "If she's done this to other men, someone needs to stop her."

"I just need you to keep quiet. If anyone finds out, it will ruin everything." I wasn't sure what he meant. "If other people know what she's doing, it's a safe bet that HR knows as well. They don't care as long as no one rocks the boat. If I complain, I'll be rocking that boat. I can't afford to get fired."

Although I didn't want to believe they would let something like this continue there had been enough news stories lately that disproved that thought. Things like this went on for years before anyone tried to stop it. Maybe I was being naïve.

"Sexual harassment is a crime, Rob." I still tried to make him see what he should do. "You can't let her get away with it."

"Do you really think anyone cares? We're both adults, so no one sees anything wrong with what she's doing. I need this job. If you go HR, and it gets out, Jill will find out. It will ruin everything, and I can't let that happen. Stay out of it. Please." He hurried away. At least he didn't threaten me this time.

She had threatened his job. I didn't want to believe no one would care. That's how sexual predators get away with their crimes for so long. He kept saying it would ruin everything, but I wasn't sure what he meant. The victim shouldn't be condemned for giving in to the threats, but it happened all the time.

Shirley was sitting in the break room going over some papers when I went in to grab a snack between patients. I hesitated when she looked up, uncertain what she would do. I started to back out, but she stopped me. "I've been meaning to talk to you, Pattiann. Have a seat." She pushed a chair out with her foot.

Reluctantly, I sat down on the edge of the chair ready to leap up if she tried to do anything to me. She set the papers aside. "What you saw yesterday isn't what you think."

"Really." I waited to see what she had to say for herself.

"Yes, really." For a long moment we were in a staring contest.

"I know you've been harassing him. I guess he finally gave in to your demands."

Her face darkened, and she leaned closer to me. "That's a pretty nasty word that could ruin careers. I don't think you want something like that on your conscience. We're two consenting adults. There is nothing wrong with what we did. Unless you're a prude, that is." She made it sound like an indictment against me. "I don't want you spreading any gossip around." It was a warning.

Hoping she was finished with me, I started to get up. But I wasn't that lucky. "Your sister-in-law owns one of the wineries around here, right?" Unsure where she was going with this, I nodded. "I heard that you work for her on your days off."

"Um, yes, I help her out, but I don't actually work there." This felt like a trap. "My step-father is Sky's partner, and my brother is married to Sky. It's sort of a family thing."

"Yes, I know all about that. Did you get permission from HR before taking a second job?"

"It's not really a job, I just help her out. She doesn't pay me."

"You still should have mentioned it to HR before you started working there." She paused for a moment. "I won't say anything as long as things remain as they are. Are we clear on what I'm saying?"

"As clear as glass. You're threatening my job if I say anything about what you're doing."

She gave a humorless laugh. "I wouldn't put it quite so bluntly as that, but you get my drift."

I stood up to leave. My hands were shaking with suppressed anger. I wanted to say more, but I knew enough to keep my mouth shut for a change.

She smiled up at me, her demeanor completely changed now that she was finished threatening me. "I've been meaning to visit some of the wineries. I've heard good things about them. Which ones would you recommend?"

If she thinks she can threaten me one minute, and be my friend the next, she was wrong. I wasn't going to play that game with her. If she wanted to know anything about the different wineries, she'd have to visit them. "They're all very good. You could try a few each weekend." I certainly hoped she didn't come out to Sky Vineyards while I was there. I'd probably end up pouring a bottle over her head instead of in a glass.

"Sounds good," she smiled, lifting one shoulder in a shrug. "Maybe I'll see you this weekend." She'd made her point, and I was being dismissed. She picked up the papers she'd been reading when I walked in. She'd accomplished what she wanted, and was done with me. Leaving without my bag of granola, I made good my escape. I was no longer hungry. I was afraid if I ate anything it would come right back up. She was a bully. The only way to handle a bully is to call their bluff. That was exactly what I planned on doing.

Heading for the administration wing on my lunch hour, I was determined to get this settled before Shirley tried to get me fired. It wasn't as complicated as I feared. Nor was it a big deal. "As long as you aren't working in competition to the hospital, there isn't a problem," Linda said. As head of the HR department, I knew she would have all the answers. "I've seen you at Sky's place several times. Did someone say something that has you worried?"

"Um…not exactly. I just wanted to make sure. Some employers don't like it if you work a second job."

She gave her head a shake. "There's nothing in the handbook against it, so you don't need to worry." I wasn't sure she believed me, but she didn't push the matter. "Tell Skylar I love her peach wine. My husband and I enjoy touring the different wineries several times a year, and I always keep a good supply of her peach wine at home."

"I'll be sure to tell her. Bonnie Carson is thinking of helping out at one of the wineries as well. It won't be a problem for her either, right? She isn't related to anyone." If Shirley tried to threaten her, I wanted to make sure there wouldn't be a problem.

"Nope, you're both fine." She frowned at me "If someone was giving you grief about this, you'd tell me, right?" One finely arched brow lifted slightly.

"It was mentioned that I should have checked with you before I started working there." I felt bad about the lie. She must have heard rumors about Shirley's activities. Was she trying to get me to tell her what I know? I didn't want to believe she would look the other way regarding something like sexual harassment.

Enough people knew about Shirley's activities for it not to have already reached HR. Was she waiting for someone to come forward? Giving a mental shrug, I stood up to leave, still unsure whether I was doing the right thing by remaining silent.

"Is there something else you'd like to tell me?" There was a hopeful expression on her face now. I wasn't going to say anything about Rob. I figured whatever happened with his girlfriend was on him now. He shouldn't have given in to Shirley's demands.

Guilt washed over me. I was applying a double standard to him. If the roles had been reversed, would I feel the same if a woman gave in because she felt her job was being threatened? I didn't think so.

"No, that's all." I sighed. "Maybe I'll see you at Sky Vineyards sometime." I made a hasty retreat, bumping into Rob as I hurried out the door.

"Pattiann." He gripped my arm, his fingers digging into my skin as he dragged me away from Linda's door. "What did you do? Please tell me you didn't tell her what happened." He had a pleading expression on his face.

"I didn't say anything about you or Shirley. I had my own problem to deal with." I shook off the grip he had on my arm. "By remaining silent, we're both letting her get away with this. If I witness another episode like the other day, I will report it to Linda. I don't care what you say."

"I'm the victim here, not the criminal." His voice was harsh.

"I know that! And you're in the position to stop her from doing this to anyone else."

"No, I'm not. Don't you know in cases like this the victim is usually the one that gets fired? Leave this alone." I didn't understand his reluctance to turn her in.

"That might have been the case in the past, but I don't think it would be now. There's been too much in the news lately about these kinds of cases."

"And all of them are with women or young girls being harassed, not men." His shoulders were slumped with a sense of defeat shrouding him as he walked away. Would his girlfriend really break up with him if she found out?

Shirley's smug smile each time she looked at me grated on my nerves. She thought she'd gotten away with another threat. I waited until we were alone at the desk before approaching her. I was going to enjoy wiping that superior look off her face.

"I wanted to let you know that I check with HR about that issue we talked about earlier."

Her face blanched slightly. "Wh…what are you talking about?" She had trouble getting the words out.

If I led her to believe I'd turned her in, and nothing happened, she would think HR didn't care. That would embolden her even further. I didn't want that to happen, but I wanted her to know that I was calling her bluff. "You know that little deal about me working at my sister-in-law's winery. Linda said there wasn't a problem."

"Oh, yes, I just wanted to be sure it was all right with HR. That's all."

"Of course you did," I agreed sarcastically. "It seemed that Linda was hoping I was talking about something else though. I wondered what she had in mind." Before she could say anything, I walked away feeling pretty good. The feeling didn't last long.

~~~

"What the heck?" There was a long scratch on the side of my car where someone had used a key on the paint job. Something like this was usually done by teenagers looking for mischief, or someone with a grudge. I didn't want to believe Rob would do something like that, but it was right up Shirley's alley.

"That's terrible. Who would do something like that?" Bonnie stood beside me, staring at my car.

"I don't know, but I intend to find out." I marched back inside to the security desk.

"I'm sorry that happened, Pattiann." Sam Burton shook his big head. A retired cop from New Mexico, he'd been working at the hospital for a couple of years as head of security. "I'm not sure the security cameras reach out that far." Hospital employees usually parked in the last rows so patient families didn't have to walk so far. He had followed me back to my car to assess the damage. It didn't look like I was going to get any satisfaction from security though. "I'll take a look at the tape. Maybe I'll get lucky, and see someone around your car. Do you know when it could have happened?"

"Any time today. The scratch wasn't there this morning when I came to work."

"Could be just teenagers going through the lot," he shrugged. "I can give you the name of a product that will wipe out that scratch like it was never there."

"Okay, thanks, Sam." This wasn't the result I wanted. Maybe he'd find the guilty party on the tape. It would be poetic justice if Shirley was fired for something as simple as
~~~

keying my car when she was guilty of so much more.

For the remainder of the week Rob avoided me like the plague. I couldn't decide whether he was angry that I'd gone to HR, or because he was feeling guilty about keying my car. I tried to tell him I hadn't said anything about him, but he wouldn't believe me.

Shirley's activities weren't as blatant as they had been. But until someone stood up to her, she would continue to get away with harassing anyone that she took a fancy to. I didn't hear anything from security, so they probably hadn't found anything on the tape.

~~~

There were no festivals on the upcoming weekend. That meant there wouldn't be enough business to keep everyone busy if Bonnie came with me again. I still hadn't called Chase to see if he needed help. After seeing him, or someone that looked like him, going into The Lamplighter, I was reluctant to call him. But I had promised Bonnie. I certainly wasn't going to ask if he frequented the place.

When he answered I hesitated, suddenly feeling a little embarrassed after asking about the flowers. I didn't know quite what to say. It was best to get it out there without beating around the bush. "Are you still looking for help in your tasting room?"

"Um, sure, but what will Skylar say if you come to work for me?" He seemed a little unsure of himself now.

"Oh, no, I don't mean me. My friend from work is interested in helping out on the weekends, but Skylar doesn't need anyone else."

"Does she have any experience working in a tasting room?" He sounded unsure now.

"She helped out at Sky Vineyard last weekend. I thought maybe she could help you out since you said you could use some help." Pouring wine isn't exactly rocket science, I thought. I clamped my lips shut on that thought. He wouldn't take it too kindly.
~~~

"Sure, I'm always looking for help in the tasting room. I've decided I can't do it all. Bring her by Friday morning. I'll give her a crash course on my wines."

"Thanks a lot, Chase. She's a sweet kid. I know you'll like her." Bonnie's exuberant enthusiasm always made me feel years older than her.

"Kid?" He questioned, suddenly unsure. "She's over twenty-one, right? I can't have someone underage working here."

"You don't have to worry," I assured him with a sigh. "She's of legal age. We work together at the hospital." Did he think I was trying to get him in trouble with the authorities?

Bonnie was excited about working at Templeton Vineyards. She caught on quickly, and didn't have any preconceived prejudices against the other wineries.

The lawyer or realtor had been to all the wineries in the area with only the one sale. No other vintners were willing to sell after working so hard to get established. Hopefully they would get the message and leave town.

~~~

Standing at the window of his hotel room, he rubbed the back of his neck. This was taking too long. He'd never encountered such a bunch of stubborn people in his life. When he'd wanted something in the past, money had always cleared the way.

These people couldn't be bought. It didn't seem to be about money with them. He shook his head. It was a foreign concept to him. They just wanted to make wine. He'd done his research. Wine was an up-and-coming industry, but it wasn't very profitable when you were just starting out.

To keep anyone from discovering his plans before he was ready, he had resorted to using a false identity. No one could know what he was doing until he managed to accomplish what he'd set out to do. Running his fingers through his thick hair, he released a frustrated sigh. He needed to get this finished so he could go home and tend to his real business there.
~~~

Until he had all this arranged he couldn't approach that stubborn boy. In his mind, he was still the stubborn eighteen-year-old who had thrown away his heritage for a whim. His stomach churned. Would he be grateful for all he'd done to help him? Or would he continue with that obstinate streak she had instilled in him, and walk away again?

~~~

Shirley was in high spirits when I went back to work the following week. "I wanted to tell you I took your advice."

"Oh? What advice?" I wasn't sure where she was going with this. I didn't trust her.

"I stopped at several tasting rooms while I was off. I met some fascinating people." There seemed to be a hidden meaning behind her words. "I especially enjoyed meeting the owners. They all seem really nice and friendly, one in particular." There was a gleam in her eyes now.

There were several single men working at the different wineries, along with two or three single vintners. If she started making friends outside of work, maybe she would leave the men at the hospital alone "I'm glad you enjoyed yourself."

"Yes, I certainly did. I never knew small towns could be so…" She paused. "I don't know what you'd call it. Maybe interesting?" Her smile was almost creepy. "Anyway, thanks for the suggestion. Maybe I'll stop at your sister-in-law's place to see what she has." She gave a hearty laugh. "It's time to get to work." Humming a tune, she turned away. I swear she was up to something. I just didn't know what.
~~~

CHAPTER NINE

Bonnie was moving a few personal items from her apartment over to my house each evening. By the time her lease was up, she would already be moved in. I was looking forward to having her as a roommate, but living and working together might get a little claustrophobic. We still needed to work out a few details.

"Is Chase sick?" A worried frown drew Bonnie's brows together when she came in.

"I don't think so. Why? Did he say something over the weekend?"

She shook her head. Her dark hair fell in her face, and she gave it an impatient shove. "He was leaving the hospital this morning when I pulled in. When I called out to him, he ignored me."

Like he had at the theater, I thought. What was up with him? When I took Bonnie to his place, I hadn't mentioned seeing him outside the theater or at The Lamplighter. I doubted that Bonnie had said anything to him.

"It was too early for visiting hours," she added. "I hope he's okay. It just seems like an odd time for him to see a doctor."

I agreed with that, but I had no way of knowing whether he was sick, or if something else was going on. I shrugged. "Maybe it wasn't anything important. I wouldn't worry about it." I wished I could take my own advice. There were a lot of odd things happening lately, and I didn't know what to make of them.

With the drama at the hospital, I had forgotten about George's warning that someone had followed me home. It was harder to forget that someone had been in my house. There was nothing here worth stealing. So what was the purpose of the break-in? I still hadn't said anything to Greg or Mom. I didn't want to worry her, and I didn't want to deal with Greg's big brother act. He would try to make me move in with Mom and Joe until he could figure out who had been in the house. I wasn't going to let him bully me either.

"Do you think Chase will ask me out?" Bonnie surprised me with her question as we walked to our cars that evening. Apparently she was no longer worried that he was sick. "Are you sure he didn't send you those flowers? If he has a thing for you…" Her voice trailed off.

"Heavens, no, we're just friends. If he asks you out, that's fine with me." At least I thought it was. My doubts about him were beginning to pile up. "I'm sure he didn't send the flowers. I don't know who did." A frown drew my eyebrows together. I was still puzzled over who sent them. "Maybe it was a patient thanking us for the good care he got." It was the only comfortable explanation I could come up with.

"But they were addressed to you personally," she said, "not the entire ER team. That means they were meant for you alone."

I shrugged off the unease that settled on me. "Maybe it was a patient that I helped on my own," I insisted. "Don't worry about stepping on my toes if Chase asks you out. He had no reason to send me flowers." Who was I trying to convince, me or her?

"So, do you think Chase will ask me out some time?" She switched back to her original question.

"I have no idea. I'm sorry." I shrugged. "I just don't know him well enough to predict what he'll do." I paused for a minute before going on. "Are you sure you want to go out with him?"

"Yeah, why wouldn't I? He's nice, good looking, has a steady job." She shrugged. "What else could someone want?"

"Well, it would be nice if you had some interests in common," I laughed.

"How do you find out that sort of thing if you don't go out with them?" She was right about that. She drew a deep breath. "You know I always lived with my parents." I nodded, unsure what that had to do with her wanting to go out with Chase. "Well…" She hesitated again. "The night we went out with Ty and his friends," her voice dropped to a whisper. "That was the closest I ever had to a date."

She was twenty-two years old. In this day and age it was unthinkable that she had never been on a date. "You never went on a date?" I couldn't help but sound surprised. "Why? Didn't your parents have friends with kids your age?"

"They didn't have any friends, or socialize with anyone. They didn't approve of me having any friends either. They were afraid something would happen to me. I'm not sure where that fear came from though. Every time a girl was abducted, they pointed out how dangerous the world is. It was like something bad had happened before I was born, and they were afraid of letting me out of their sight. Please don't say anything to anyone. It's embarrassing to not have been on a date at my age."

I couldn't imagine never having any friends. It did explain a lot of things though. She had no idea how to go about it on her own. I gave her a hug. "I promise not to say anything." It was no one's business.

"So, do you think I'm Chase's type?" She was all smiles again.

"I have no idea what his type is," I laughed. "You'll be working with him again this weekend, so just be friendly. But not too friendly," I cautioned. I didn't want her to get in trouble or have her heart broken. I thought of the mess Rob had gotten himself into with Shirley. I felt sorry for him, but still believed he should have reported what she was doing.

Ty's schedule was as crazy as mine, but we still managed to see each other. We both had the next two day off, and we were planning on going to dinner both nights. I kept hoping one of his friends would ask Bonnie out, but so far that hadn't happened.

While I was working, there wasn't much opportunity to talk to Mom or Sky. My evenings were taken up with getting ready for Bonnie to move in with me. I had no idea if the winery owners were still being pressed to sell.

My first day back at Sky Vineyard answered my question. Mr. Earnhardt had just gotten out of his car when I pulled down the lane. Skylar approached him before he could say anything.

"Sir, if you come here again, I'm going to have you arrested for harassment." Skylar glared at him. Cody stood between her and Mr. Earnhardt, a low growl in his throat. I'd never seen this protective side of the big Golden Retriever before.

"Miss Bishop, if you'll give…"

"It's Mrs. Wilkinson," she interrupted him. For business purposes, she used her maiden name, but for everything else she was Mrs. Wilkinson.

"Yes, of course, Mrs. Wilkinson, forgive me. I'm not harassing you. My client has increased his offer. I thought you might be interested."

"Well, I'm not. I'd like you to leave. Now!" Joe stood beside her in case the man decided not to take her advice.

"You haven't heard the offer." If he kept pushing, Joe was ready to push back. I got out of my car to stand with them.

"I'm not interested in any offer. My winery isn't for sale. Now leave." She pulled her cell phone off of her belt.

With a huff, he got back in his car. She waited until the big car turned onto the highway, before heading to the house. "I'd better warn the other owners."

A few minutes later, she was back, a confused frown drawing her brows together. "So far, no one has contacted Chase about selling his vineyard."

"Maybe they know he wouldn't sell," I suggested.

"How would they know that if they didn't stop by with an offer? He said neither of them has been by to see him." Confusion mingled with suspicion on her face.

"Could be he's behind both of those offers to buy us out," Joe grumbled. "He always had an eye on this place." He didn't like Chase. I doubted if anything would ever change that.

"If he was behind this, why would he have a lawyer and a realtor making offers?" I asked. "It seems like they're competing with each other." Joe didn't have an answer to that. When the first group of tourists pulled into the lane a few minutes later, he headed for the vineyard. He didn't want to deal with the tourists unless there was trouble.

Several hours later Bonnie called. "I did it." She said in an excited whisper. "I can't believe I actually did it."

"You did what?"

"I asked Chase to go to dinner with me."

I choked on a laugh. "Well good for you. What did he say?"

"Sort of like you, he laughed. Then he said yes." She was probably bouncing off the walls right about now.

"Oh, well, that's great. Where are you taking him?"

She giggled at that. "I told him he could choose. Oh, I have to go. We have more customers." The line went dead.

I was surprised that she'd asked him, and said a prayer that Chase would treat her nice. If he was the one trying to buy out the competition, he wasn't the nice guy I thought he was. I still didn't know if he was the man Bonnie and I had seen in town. I didn't know what difference it made either. If it was him, why hadn't he acknowledged us when I called out to him?

~~~

"Hey guys." I turned to see Greg and Sky had followed us through the door at Manuel's Mexican Restaurant that evening. "Fancy meeting you here." Skylar laughed at the surprise on my face. "This is our favorite restaurant, too."

"Four for dinner?" the hostess asked, holding up the menus.

"Um," I looked at Greg. I didn't want to spend the evening with him if he was going to pull his big brother act again.

"Sounds good," Greg said, reaching around Sky to shake Ty's hand. It looked like he was on good-behavior tonight.
~~~

The hostess started to lead us to a table when I heard someone call my name. Bonnie and Chase were at a table next to the one she was leading us to. I groaned inwardly. This would be worse than Greg's big brother act. He and Chase didn't get along.

Unaware of the undercurrent, the hostess turned with a smile. "Is this table okay?" She started setting down the menus.

Greg looked like a thundercloud ready to pour down rain. "This is fine," Skylar said, forcing a smile. "Right, dear." She poked her husband with her elbow. The tables weren't connected, but were close enough that we could carry on a conversation together if we chose.

"Right." He nodded agreement as he rubbed his side where her elbow had connected with his ribs.

Chase didn't seem any happier about the seating arrangement than Greg was. He looked resigned to an uncomfortable evening though when we sat down. Greg took the chair farthest away from Chase as possible. The uncomfortable tension confused Bonnie and Ty. She knew part of the history between Chase and Skylar, but didn't know where Greg came into the picture. Ty was completely in the dark.

Although Bonnie didn't have any experience dating in high school and college, she was eager to get started. In spite of being sheltered all those years, she wasn't shy. She was eager to meet people and make friends. Even Greg and Chase couldn't resist her bubbly personality. Before dinner was over, we were all visiting back and forth. The two men seemed to get along, even though they would never be best of friends.

When the check was placed on their table, both Bonnie and Chase reached for it. When Chase won, she leaned across the table. "I asked you out, that means I pay," she whispered.

Giving his head a shake, he smiled at her. "Not where I came from. Besides, this has been one of the best evenings I've had in a while."

His eyes slide over to me, causing my heart to thump uncomfortably in my chest. It wouldn't be good if he announced right here that we'd shared a meal recently. When he didn't say anything further, I released the breath I was holding. Hopefully, no one else had been paying attention to that exchange. We parted ways outside the restaurant. Dinner was one thing, but extending the evening further wasn't going to happen.

Sitting on the porch at my house, I handed Ty a bottle of beer while I had a glass of wine. The night was cool, but I didn't mind. Ty was beside me with his arm draped over my shoulder. I was plenty warm.

"Would you like to explain what happened when we first sat down? I thought for a minute Greg was going to go all big brother on Chase. You and Bonnie aren't related, are you?"

"No," I sighed. "There's some bad blood between Greg and Chase. It's a really long story."

"How about giving me the Cliff Notes version then?" There didn't seem to be a way around explaining, but I kept it short.

"Do you think Chase is behind the offers to buy the vineyards around here?" He managed to jump right to the heart of the latest problem when I finished explaining.

"No, I don't think Chase is that underhanded. Unfortunately, Greg and Joe don't share my opinion. Skylar is reserving judgment until more facts are in. We don't know who is trying to buy up the different properties. That's what is driving the speculation. I don't understand the need for secrecy, unless something underhanded is going on," I added.

"For Bonnie's sake, I hope he isn't involved," Ty said.

I silently agreed with him. I didn't want to see her get hurt. If he was involved, I didn't see any way around it though.

It was late when Ty left, and I struggled to get up in time for church Sunday morning. Because the tasting rooms in the area were open on Sunday, the different churches held an early service so those working could go to church before it was time to open. That meant a short night after Ty left.

To my surprise, Bonnie was waiting for me when I walked up to the door. A huge smile spread across her face. "I had so much fun last night," she whispered. "Chase is a really nice guy."

"I'm glad you had fun. Just don't get hooked on the first guy you go out with," I warned. "There are a lot of fish in the sea, even though the sea in New Haven is small."

"Oh, you." Her cheeks turned pink at my reminder. She had been convinced there were no single men in our small town. Now she'd met several. I just wish Walt would call her so she wouldn't settle on the first guy that treated her nice.

The tasting room closes early on Sunday. People that come from different parts of the state usually head home shortly after three depending on how far they have to drive. I was almost ready for Bonnie to move in with me, but there were still a few things I needed to pack away.

I kept watch on my rearview mirror as I left Sky Vineyards. Only once had I thought someone was following me. But I had been driving too slowly that night. My mind had been on other matters. I kept hoping George had been wrong the night I had dinner with Chase.

It was becoming a habit to check each door, window, and room each time I came home. Nothing was ever out of place.

Someone had only been in my house that one time. I was certain of it. I told myself that I'd interrupted them before they could take anything. As a precaution, I watched my credit report in case whoever broke in tried to set up any phony accounts. So far nothing had happened.

Rob continued to avoid me for which I was glad. He still believed that I'd told Linda about what had happened between him and Shirley. The fact that HR hadn't called him to ask about it was further evidence to him they didn't care about what she was doing.

Shirley hadn't made any further advances towards him or anyone else that I knew about. I wanted no part of what she was doing, but I promised myself that if I had any direct knowledge of her activities, I'd report it immediately this time. I didn't care what Rob said. What she was doing was a big deal. And it was illegal.

"That woman is absolutely insufferable," Martha grumbled. She was still upset that Shirley got the job instead of her.

"What's she done now?" If it involved anyone at the hospital, I wasn't sure I wanted to know.

"She's bragging about the new man in her life. She said he owns a 'prestigious' local winery." She made air quotes around the word. "She keeps dropping hints like she wants people to ask who he is. But when they do, she acts like it's a big secret. Like I really care." She gave a sniff of disdain.

Why all the secrecy? I wondered. If she was really dating one of the owners, it wouldn't take long for the news to spread. There were only so many single men in the category she was talking about. Chase came to mind. I didn't think she was exactly his type, but what did I know.

"Why the big mystery?" I asked, hoping she had an answer.

Martha shrugged. "It makes her look more important, at least in her own eyes. Supposedly the man is in some sort of negotiations over something. I think it's all a lie to bolster her own self-image." She stomped off.

"P-P-Pattiann," George stopped me as I was getting ready to leave that evening. "You n-n-need to be careful." It had been several days since I'd seen him around the hospital.

"Slow down, and tell me what you mean." Butterflies began to flutter in my stomach. "Take a deep breath." Since the night he came to tell me someone had followed me home from the diner he had been extra jumpy.

"I been watching, and that guy's still following you." As long as he remembered to use a sing-song voice his stutter disappeared. "You have to be careful."

"What guy? Are you talking about the man I was with at

the diner?" My voice shook slightly. It had been more than two weeks since I had dinner with Chase.

He didn't answer right away. "Sort of," he finally answered. He looked around like he thought someone was going to jump out at him.

"What do you mean, sort of? Either it is or it isn't." Was he making this up for some reason?

A puzzled frown drew his bushy brows together like he didn't understand my question. Finally giving his head a shake, he lifted his shoulders in a shrug at the same time. "It could be. You need to be careful." Before I could ask any more questions, he hurried off.

A chill moved up my spine. I watched him disappear through the automatic doors. Four days off sounded really good right about now.

CHAPTER TEN

"I heard that Shirley is dating one of the winery owners," Bonnie whispered as we headed for our cars that evening. "She said he was a big shot in the wine community. Do you think it's Chase? He hasn't called me since I asked him out for dinner." Her usual smile was absent. "Maybe I was too forward. My mom always said men didn't like women to be pushy."

"We don't know who she's dating," I reminded her. "But I wouldn't worry about it. If Shirley is going out with Chase, he isn't your type, not the other way around. The right guy is out there for you. Just relax and enjoy yourself." She needed more dating experience before she settled on one guy.

Her tinkling laugh drifted on the balmy night air. "I know, and I'm going to have fun finding him. Ty's friend Walt called me today." She was no longer worried about Chase. She did a little happy dance. Oh, to be that young again, I thought with a laugh. Two years separated us. It might as well be twenty. I wondered when I'd lost the innocence she displayed.

"I was afraid he wasn't going to call me, but he said he'd been out of town. He asked me to go out with him on a real date. We're going out tonight. Have you heard from Ty?"

I was happy for her. "We went out the other night. He's really busy with his job, and he's still in the Reserves."

"Well, maybe he'll call you this weekend. I gotta hurry," she giggled. "I'll see you tomorrow." She was in a rush to get ready for her date with Walt.

When my phone buzzed, I pulled it out of my pocket, keeping my fingers crossed that it would be Ty. Seeing an unknown number, I almost let it go to voice mail. At the last minute, I answered. I hadn't programed Ty's number into my phone yet. Maybe it was him.

"Hi, Pattiann. Are you still at work?"

My heart skipped a beat. It was Ty. "I'm leaving the

hospital right now."

"Could I talk you into meeting me somewhere for dinner?"

"What the heck?" I stopped beside my car where a single rose was tucked under the windshield wiper. I looked around to see if anyone was watching me.

"Huh? You don't want to have dinner with me?"

"No, I mean yes I want to have dinner with you. I was talking about something else. What did you have in mind?" I wasn't successful at keeping the quiver out of my voice. Thankfully, Ty didn't pursue the matter. I pulled the flower off the windshield, and tossed it on the ground, stomping on it for good measure.

"How about trying that new Italian place that just opened up?" Thanks to the mayor's efforts to grow New Haven's tourist industry, several new restaurants had recently opened.

Agreeing to meet there, I pulled out of the parking spot. I kept a sharp eye out for anyone lurking in the shadows. There wasn't anyone around.

~~~

He watched from the shadows as she got to her car. She was distracted by the phone call, but the rose quickly drew her attention. He chuckled when she tossed the flower on the ground and stomped on it. Her eyes swept the parking lot. She was spooked. She was also angry. He'd debated whether to add a note, but it was better to keep her guessing.

His original plans had morphed into something a little more sinister. Until he could figure out his next move, he was going to enjoy this new direction.

He felt like a movie director, plotting what the actors in his little drama were going to do. As long as things went his way, he'd go with the flow. There was still that other little beauty he could play with, and see where it would go. He couldn't let this continue too much longer though.

As she left the parking lot, an old car fell in behind her. Was it a coincidence, or was someone else following her? Falling in behind the old car, he decided to find out where
~~~

they were going. They made a neat little caravan going down the street together.

Instead of following her into the parking lot of a restaurant, the old car parked across the street. He couldn't see who was driving. Unless he interfered with his plans, it really didn't matter.

As she got out of her car, some guy met her with a kiss. Things might be looking up after all. He chuckled to himself. Two motives for murder are love and money. Jealousy would work out just fine.

~~~

"Why were you upset when I called?" Ty waited until the hostess seated us at a table before asking his question. Even this late on a Wednesday evening the restaurant was busy. He kept his voice low so the others couldn't eavesdrop on us.

"Oh, it was nothing important. How was your day?" I tried to deflect him, but it didn't work.

"It was important enough to distract you from our conversation." Reaching across the table to take my hand, he raised his eyebrows as he waited for me to answer.

"There was something on my windshield. That's all. See no big deal." I shrugged.

"An advertisement?" He was frowning now. "Why would that upset you?"

I sighed. He wasn't going to give up until he got a satisfactory answer. "It wasn't an advertisement. Someone put a flower under my wiper blade." It suddenly dawned on me that he might have left it. "Did you put the rose there?" I was going to be very embarrassed if he had.

"No," he frowned. "Who would leave a flower on your car? Am I cutting in on someone else's territory by asking you out?"

"No, of course not. If I was dating someone, I wouldn't have accepted your invitations."

"Okay, so who left you the flower?"

"I have no idea." That was the truth. He waited silently for
~~~

me to explain. Police use a prolonged silence to make a suspect nervous. Before long they begin to spill their guts to fill that silence. I understood that concept now. I was getting nervous. I didn't want to start babbling, but how did I explain the rose and why I was upset by it?

Seeing no way around it, I went with the short version, explaining about the flowers sent to the hospital. "I don't know who sent them. It was just the one time. I was beginning to think they had been delivered to me in error. Until tonight," I added softly. I left out the part about being followed, and someone being in my house. That would open a whole other can of worms. George's recent warning had me on edge, but I wasn't certain he'd been right about that.

"What does Greg say about it?"

I almost laughed. "How do you think Greg would react if he knew someone was sending me flowers anonymously?"

"So what you're saying is that you haven't told him." He squeezed my hand when I didn't answer.

"It's really nothing to worry about. He's so busy with his job I don't want to bother him. I'd appreciate it if you wouldn't say anything either." I picked up the menu when the server approached our table.

I settled on an antipasto salad. This conversation was already giving me indigestion. A heavy meal of pasta this late in the day would only make it worse. When we were alone again, Ty picked up the conversation where we'd left off.

"I think Greg would want to know about this. It sounds like someone is stalking you. That could be dangerous."

My stomach churned uncomfortably. Stalking sounded a lot more serious than saying someone was following me. "It's just flowers," I tried to argue, but there was no conviction in my voice. The butterflies in my stomach were beginning to riot.

"Right now it's just flowers. If someone is stalking you, it will escalate and get dangerous." There was that word again. I didn't want to think about it. "Is there an ex-boyfriend who wants to get back together? Someone who asked you out, but you rejected?" He lifted one eyebrow in question.

"No, I haven't been dating anyone for several months. It was a mutual decision when my last boyfriend and I parted company." His questions were making me nervous.

"Sexual harassment is usually a man's game. Has one of the doctors made any advances towards you?" He wasn't going to let this go. How much did he know about Shirley's activities?

"No. Now can we forget this and enjoy our dinner?" My voice was a little testy. He was grilling me like Greg would a suspect. The waiter delivered our food, giving me an excuse to call a halt to the interrogation.

"Okay, sorry. I'll just say one more thing before I drop the subject. I really do think you need to tell Greg. The fact that this guy knows where you work is a little disturbing."

He also knows where I live, and how to get in my house, I thought, keeping that to myself.

~~~

How long does it take them to eat dinner? He looked at his watch. They'd been in there an hour and a half. This isn't some five-star restaurant where you're served a seven-course dinner. Dinner usually led to more interesting pursuits. He didn't want to miss out on that, but he was getting bored. He was also becoming uncomfortable. He needed to relieve himself before much longer. Going somewhere wasn't an option though. That would be the time she left the restaurant.

The guy in the beater hadn't moved either. Maybe he'd come prepared with a bottle, or something. It would be interesting to know what was up with him. Was he stalking her, or was he spying on her for some other reason?

When they finally walked out, he gave a sigh of relief. Now if they would only go back to her place.

~~~

It was close to nine o'clock when we left the restaurant. Once we dropped the subject of the flowers, it had been a pleasant dinner. The restaurant was still busy, and the parking lot was crowded. New Haven wasn't a hub of activity after dark, but the restaurants in town stayed busy on most nights. Most stores closed earlier so the employees could spend time with their families though.

Leaning against the side of my car, Ty pulled me into his arms. His head dipped to capture my lips. It was several minutes before he lifted his head. "I'll follow you home," he whispered.

"That isn't…"

He placed his finger over my lips. "If someone is stalking you, I want to make sure you're safe." He stepped back, taking my keys from my hand. Clicking the key fob, he held my car door open for me.

"What are your plans for tomorrow? Sky isn't open, is she?"

I shook my head. "I have things to do around the house to finish getting ready for Bonnie to move in. I'm looking forward to having a roommate again."

He chuckled. "Walt said he called Bonnie, and she told him the same thing. The two of you make a good pair. He's rather stuck on her." Giving me another kiss, he stepped back. "My truck is right over there." He pointed at the big red truck. "I'll follow you." He closed the door before I could argue.

"Wow," I whispered. My mind was jumping with thoughts of where this could lead. Checking my rearview mirror, I backed out. Ty's truck stayed right behind me.

He pulled up to the curb when I pulled into my driveway. Before I could gather my work things, he was at my door holding it open for me. He took my hand to help me out. My stomach fluttered as he placed a kiss on my lips. "I'd feel better if you'd let me check your house before you go in." Now he was making me really nervous.

"That's not necessary, I promise. I make sure the doors and windows are locked before I leave each morning. Greg installed dead bolts when Mom and I first moved in. There shouldn't be a way for anyone to get inside." There shouldn't be, I thought, but someone had been able to get in. I couldn't tell him that though. If he checked the house out, it would be hard to explain about the chair I still kept propped under the door knob on the back door.

For several beats, I thought he was going to argue. He finally sighed. "All right." Lacing his fingers through mine, he walked me to the door. Standing under the porch light, he pulled me into his arms. Resting his forehead against mine, he looked down at me, "This has been fun without the whole gang along." He joked about the night all of his buddies went out with Bonnie and me. "I'm off tomorrow. Would you like to do something tomorrow night? Or am I monopolizing your time?"

My heart was banging against my ribs. "If you are, I'm not complaining." This one was a keeper.

Taking the keys from my hand, he unlocked the door. With a final kiss, he stepped back. "Lock the door when you get in. See you tomorrow." He looked over his shoulder at the cars down the street. He was being overly cautious, but I didn't argue. Stepping inside, I peeked out at him, before closing the door. "Lock it," he instructed. His voice was a little strained.

Going to the window, I watched him drive away. Something had made him nervous, but I didn't understand what. Within seconds, an old car slowly rolled past. A familiar-looking truck followed a few seconds later. I couldn't see a logo on the side, but I would swear it was the same kind of truck Chase drives. My heart climbed into my throat. Why would he be following Ty? Following us?

An uneasy sensation settled over me. Pulling my cell phone from my purse, I scrolled down to the number of the call as I left the hospital. "Ty, someone is following you." I was almost shouting. "Be careful." Something wasn't right. Was Chase following me? Why would he do that? It was the same kind of truck that had followed me home the night I went to ask if he'd sent the flowers.

"It's okay, Pattiann. I saw the car, but he's not back there now. He turned off."

"What about the truck?"

There was a pause, probably while he checked his rearview mirror. "There's no one behind me. I'm okay. Keep your doors locked. If you see a truck out front, it will be mine. I'm not leaving you alone tonight."

"You can't sleep in your truck all night," I objected.

"I've slept in worse places, and who said I'd be sleeping anyway. If someone is stalking you, I'm going to make sure you're safe. You might want to reconsider telling Greg about what's going on. He isn't going to like it if you keep this from him."

My stomach rolled at that. If I told him now, it would be bad enough. If I waited, it would be worse. Still, I didn't want to go running to my big brother at what might turn out to be nothing. "You don't have to stay in your truck," I said into the uneasy silence. "You can sleep on the couch. I'm sure that will be more comfortable."

He gave a bark of laughter. "Think about what you just said. What would Greg's reaction be to that even if I'm on the couch? I'd like to live a few more years. Get some sleep. I'll see you tomorrow."

I reluctantly put down my phone. Going to the window, I pulled the blinds back enough to peek out. Ty's truck was sitting out front. The headlights flashed once to let me know he'd seen me. I knew he was right. Greg would imagine the worst if Ty slept in the house with me.

I went around checking the doors and windows. I'd be glad when Bonnie was here with me. Or was I getting her into a dangerous situation? I didn't know the answer to that.

George's warning was making me paranoid. Was someone really following me? Or was George making it up? I didn't know why he would do something like that. His explanation that it was 'sort of' the guy I'd been with at the diner didn't make sense. What did he mean? Had the person in the car and truck been following us? Or was it a coincidence that they left at the same time Ty had? My thoughts were going in circles. It took a long time to fall asleep that night.

~~~

He was disappointed when the guy in the truck didn't follow her inside. Too bad he hadn't thought about planting a couple of cameras in her house while he was in there. He could still do that, but first things first. He needed to figure out who the guy in the beater car was. What was his game? If he got in the way, he'd have to take him out. That thought didn't bother him. In fact, it might be fun.

His new plan was beginning to take shape in his mind. He wasn't going to allow anything to interfere. She was in for the night. There was nothing more to see. He turned at the next corner. It was time to get some sleep.

~~~

When I got up the next morning, Ty's truck was gone. The street was empty. Last evening seemed like a dream, a bad one. I didn't want to believe someone was stalking me. By the middle of the afternoon I was through with all my chores. The house was clean, and ready for Bonnie to move in. I usually spend most of my days off at the winery with Skylar. It was time to give her a break. She hadn't been used to having a shadow until I came into her life.

When Ty showed up, he looked well rested. If he'd spent the night on guard duty outside my house, it didn't show on his face now. Maybe he'd taken a nap this afternoon. I didn't want to spoil the mood by bringing up the night before, so I didn't ask.

Instead of going out, I'd spent the afternoon cooking. If someone was following me, they were going to be disappointed tonight. I wasn't going anywhere. "Something smells good." Ty sniffed the cinnamon-scented air. After placing a soft kiss on my lips, he stepped back. "Is that something you're cooking, or your shampoo?" He sniffed my hair.

"When I cook, I tend to get spices everywhere," I said sheepishly. "I made apple crisp, adding a few touches of my own to an old standby recipe."

"If it tastes half as good as you smell, I can't wait to taste it." He placed another kiss on my lips. Stepping back, he followed me into the kitchen, his arm draped over my shoulder. "I thought we were going out. I didn't mean for you to go to the trouble of cooking."

"It's no trouble, I love to cook and experiment. You're getting one of my experiments tonight. I hope we don't end up in the emergency room," I teased.

"Has that ever happened?" He pretended to be appalled by the prospect.

"No, but there's always a first time." The evening was fun, without any talk of being followed, or flowers from a mysterious admirer. I had a large selection of DVD movies, and we managed to watch two before we were both ready to fall asleep on the couch.

"I think I'd better go." He stood up, stretching his arms wide. I enjoyed watching the muscles move under the fabric of his snug-fitting shirt. Pulling me into his arms, his kiss rocked me to the soles of my feet.

With a final kiss, he unlocked the door, stepping out on the porch. He scanned the empty street. If anyone had been watching my house, they got bored and left a long time ago. "Maybe I'll see you at the winery tomorrow. There are still a few of Skylar's wines I haven't sampled. Stay inside," he said as I started to follow him out. "Lock the door." He pulled the door shut, waiting to hear the lock click into place.

~~~

He looked down at the woman's body on the bed. It had been fun while it lasted, he thought. This wasn't how he had imagined the night to end. Somehow things had gotten out of hand when she started asking questions. What had given him away? How had she known? Had she guessed the truth, or
~~~

had he said something to tip her off? His thoughts were racing around in his mind. When she threatened to tell, he had no other choice but to silence her permanently.

He paced across the room until he bumped into the wall. "What the hell?" he muttered, coming up short. Looking around at the small room, he shook his head in disgust. His closet at home was bigger than the bedroom, almost bigger than the entire apartment. How did people live like this? He shuddered at the thought.

Practical matters crowded in on his thoughts. The empty wine bottle and two glasses were good props. But he needed to remove his fingerprints from every surface he'd touched. He hadn't planned for the evening to end this way, or he would have come prepared.

With his mind racing, he sat down on the edge of the bed ignoring the fact there was a dead woman beside him. First, he needed to wipe away any evidence that he'd ever been here. Second, he needed to make it look like someone else had done this. He debated whether to leave her here or dispose of her somewhere else. She had bragged about their big date. The hints she dropped could lead to any number of men. How could he use that to his advantage?

A plan began to crystalize in his mind. With a laugh, he stood up. He knew what he needed to do. This was going to be a long night, but that was okay. He could sleep in the morning.

CHAPTER ELEVEN

Shirley made a point of being at the desk each morning, keeping track of anyone coming in late. It was her way to let everyone know she was in charge. The fact that she wasn't there when I arrived seemed odd, but I didn't let it worry me. Maybe her big date wore her out, and she'd be late for a change.

"I guess she isn't so perfect after all," Martha gloated. It was nine-thirty and Shirley still hadn't come in. She hadn't called either. That was completely out of character. "She made a point of telling anyone who would listen that her weekend was going to be devoted to the new man in her life."

"Did she say who she was going out with?"

"She's still being very mysterious. All she'd say is that he's someone important around here. I don't believe that for a minute. She's desperate if she has to threaten men in order to get them to sleep with her. She'd say anything to make herself look important." She stomped off, still angry that Shirley had gotten the job of head nurse instead of her.

Sexual harassment wasn't about the sex, I reminded myself. It was about power. If Shirley was on a power trip, she wouldn't stop harassing the male employees under her charge simply because she had a new man in her life. I didn't understand why Martha hadn't gone to HR with what she knew or suspected. It would be a good way to rid herself of her rival.

By mid-morning Shirley still hadn't shown up. Everyone was speculating on where she was. "Don't you think you should call her?" I asked Martha. "She could be sick."

"Or she could be having the time of her life with her latest boy toy. She wouldn't thank me for interrupting her. I'm not getting involved."

"But it isn't like her to not show up. Wouldn't she at least call to say she wasn't coming in?" If nothing else, I thought she wouldn't want to lose her job over a one-night stand.

Martha shrugged. "She wouldn't do the same for one of us. She'd just fire us on the spot." That was probably what she was hoping would happen. She wanted Shirley's job.

When my phone buzzed with an incoming text, I pulled it from my pocket. I don't make a habit of checking my phone while I'm working, but something told me this one was important. The 9-1-1 text was from Skylar. My heart leaped into my throat. Law enforcement officers have a target on their back in recent years. Even in a small county there are crimes where police get injured or worse.

"Please God, keep Greg safe," I whispered as I slipped into the break room. I hit her number, and she answered before it finished ringing the first time. "What happened? Is Greg all right?" I didn't give her a chance to say hello.

"Calm down, Greg is fine. It's..." She paused, having trouble telling me what the emergency was, and my imagination was spinning out of control. There was any number of scenarios where someone I loved could be hurt. Mom worked in a bank. A bank robbery gone wrong could have deadly consequences. "Chase called before Greg left this morning." She interrupted my whirling thoughts. "Someone had been to his place during the night."

Relief almost brought me to my knees. "What do you mean been to his place? Did someone break-in?" That was better than where my imagination had taken me, but I didn't see why that constituted a 9-1-1 text. "Is he all right? Was anything taken?"

"Um, no, not exactly. He said it looked like someone had a picnic on his front porch. A couple of his workers found a woman's body in the vineyard." My knees buckled, and I grabbed the back of the chair to keep from falling down.

"Oh my gosh. What happened? Who is it?" My mind immediately went to Shirley. She still hadn't shown up.

"That's what Greg is trying to find out. I just wanted to let you know in case Ty brings the body into the morgue." The morgue was in the basement of the hospital. It was logical that one of the paramedics would be bringing the body here.

"How did she die? Why was she in Chase's vineyard?" My mind was reeling. The fact that Shirley had bragged about having a big date with one of the vineyard owners stuck in my mind.

Skylar sighed. "You know your brother. He hasn't said anything, but Juan Garcia talked to the guys who found the body. She was naked. It looked like she had bruises around her neck." Juan had worked for Skylar for several years, and was hoping to have his own vineyard someday.

"She was murdered?" I whispered, even as I realized it was a dumb question. A naked woman wouldn't wander into the vineyard, and have a heart attack or something. "Does Greg think Chase killed her?" Another dumb question. Chase would be a suspect simply because the woman was found on his property. "Do you know who she is?"

"From what the workers told Juan, there was nothing but the body out there. Greg's team is still working the scene. I haven't talked to him, so I don't know any details. I haven't talked to Chase either. I think Greg is still questioning him."

Knowing how the two men felt about each other, I didn't think that would go very well. "The news will get around soon enough, just don't say anything. You'll probably be hearing a lot of gossip, and I didn't want you to worry. Come out when you get off work."

That's exactly what I would be doing. Shirley was still missing, or at least not at work. Someone should check on her.

New Haven was no different from any other small town where news travels with the speed of lightning. By the time the paramedics brought the woman's body to the morgue, speculation was high. It didn't take long after that for the news to get around the hospital that Shirley had been murdered. "I didn't like her, and I didn't want her here," Martha whispered to me, "but I didn't want her dead either. I can't believe Chase would do something like that." The locals know all the vineyard owners, but Chase kept to himself most of the time. Martha made it sound like she was familiar with him in particular.

"How well do you know Chase?" I asked. Divorced, with a teenage son and a preteen daughter, she made no bones about looking for a new man in her life. She didn't try forcing them to have sex with her though. At least I didn't think she did.

"I've been out to his tasting room several times if that's what you mean. He's always friendly. He doesn't come into town very often though." A frown wrinkled her forehead. "At least not until recently," she added. "I've seen him around a couple of times lately." She got quiet. "He walked right past me the last time I saw him. It's like he's a different person when he comes to town. If someone speaks to him, he answers, but he doesn't stick around to chat."

That sounded familiar. I'd been sure it was Chase leaving the movie theater. But when I called out to him he hurried away.

"She said she had a big date. Did she give you any indication who she was seeing?" I'd asked her this once before, but I asked again.

She shook her head. "It's not like we were friends or anything. She didn't confide in me. I just heard her saying she had a big date with someone important." She lifted her shoulders in a shrug. "That's all I know. I'll see you later." She hurried off before I could ask any more questions. That wasn't the way she'd explained it before. How much of what she said was the truth?

"I thought Chase was a nice guy," Bonnie whispered. She was understandably upset by the news. The fact that she worked alone with him in the tasting room had her spooked now. "How could he kill someone?"

"We don't know that he did, Bonnie. Greg is just getting started on the investigation."

"But she was found in his vineyard. Why would someone

else kill her there?" I didn't have an answer for her.

"He's innocent until proven guilty," I reminded her. "Greg will figure this out." Why would Chase kill her, and leave her in his own vineyard? That made no sense. He wasn't that stupid.

Rob followed me out when I left that night. He looked relieved, not upset. "I'm sorry she's dead," he voiced the same sentiment as Martha had earlier. "But it takes me off the hook." When HR hadn't called him in after my visit to see Linda, he forgot about being mad at me. He looked down at me now. "I know that sounds rather cold-hearted, but I can't help it. She wasn't a very nice person. Maybe she tried to threaten or blackmail that guy, and this is what happened." He shook his head.

"Chase would never do anything like that," I argued.

"But you think I would?" He lifted an eyebrow. His anger returned.

"I didn't say that. She might still be alive if you'd gone to HR with what she was doing."

"There you go blaming the victim again. I didn't do anything to her. Try to remember she was harassing me, not the other way around."

"I know that, but no matter what she did, she didn't deserve to be murdered." He gave a careless shrug, but didn't say anything. "Do you know who else she had been harassing?" I asked.

He frowned at me now. "I'm not telling you anything, Pattiann. I told you once to leave it alone, and you couldn't do that. I'll say it again. Leave this alone. It doesn't concern you."

"It concerns everyone. She worked with us, and someone murdered her."

"Not my problem. Stop poking your nose where it doesn't belong. Some people won't take kindly to having their names dragged through the mud. That includes me."

"Are you threatening me again?" What was going on

around here? No matter what she'd done, she didn't deserve to be murdered and her naked body left in a vineyard.

He didn't bother to answer me as he stomped off. Had she continued pressing him to have sex with her? Could he have killed her to make her stop? A shiver moved down my spine. These were people I worked with. I thought I knew them. How could I have been so blind?

A lot of people already had Chase tried, convicted, and put away for life. It wasn't right. For Chase's sake, I hoped Greg was able to find the killer quickly.

"What can you tell me about her?" Greg started questioning me as soon as I got out of my car that evening. Ty had been the paramedic on duty that morning, and had given a tentative identification. I didn't know anything about her personal life. I hoped he wouldn't expect me to do the final identification. I'd seen dead bodies in the course of my work. But this would be different. I'd never seen a murder victim before.

Cody nosed up to me, looking for some attention. Taking time to rough up his ears, I tried to decide what to say. "She hasn't been at the hospital very long. I don't know that much about her."

"I can get that from her personnel file. I need to know more about the woman. Did she have friends at the hospital? Did she have a problem with anyone?" He kept pushing as we sat down on the porch.

"I think a few of the other nurses were upset that she got the job of head nurse instead of them." I was trying to give him information without actually giving him names.

"All right, I haven't talked to her co-workers yet. What else? I know there's something else you aren't telling me." How much had Ty said about Shirley's activities at the hospital?

Anything I said could cause problems for Rob, and maybe others. I didn't know how to avoid that though. If her actions had anything to do with her death, Greg needed to know. Half of my mind said to keep silent while the other half said to tell what I know. Rob's response to the news of Shirley's death still bothered me. His actions not only affected him, but his girlfriend as well. Had he been so worried she'd find out that he'd snapped?

"Earth to Pattiann," Greg snapped his fingers in front of my face bringing me back from my internal argument. Mom always knew when I told a lie. Even leaving things out doesn't work for me. I finally repeated what Shirley had said to me, trying to leave Rob out of the mix. "She threatened you because you help out around here? What difference does that make? What aren't you telling me?" Now we got to the hard part.

I sighed. "I think she was harassing some of the men at the hospital."

"Harassing how?" One eyebrow lifted slightly. When I didn't say anything, he continued. "You think she was, or you know she was." He let the silence draw out.

"I know she was." I sighed.

"Did you catch them?"

"Heavens no!" My face was getting hot.

He chuckled at my response, but grew serious once again. "How do you know for sure?" He was going to keep pushing for more information. Rob wasn't going to be happy with me.

"I heard her talking with someone. She promised she would make sure he got a position at the hospital when he graduates in a few months." The words left a bad taste in my mouth.

"Sexual harassment is a pretty good motive. Who was she harassing?" I sighed. There was no way around it. I had to give him Rob's name. I felt like a traitor. That's how Rob would see it. "Do you know if he gave in to her demands?"

Betraying Rob left me feeling miserable, but I had little choice. I nodded my head. "That's when she sort of threatened my job because I work here."

"Was she harassing anyone else?"

"I have no direct knowledge of that," I said truthfully.

"But you've heard things," he prompted again.

"Isn't that hearsay?" I was getting very uncomfortable with this conversation.

"This isn't a trial. Tell me what you've heard. I'll follow up to see if there's anything to it."

I gave a sigh. "There were rumors about her and other men. Before you ask, I don't know who. She might have propositioned some of the paramedics." He nodded his head at that. Ty had been at the scene, so he probably already told Greg this. "If you already knew about this, why are you pressing me for answers?"

"I have to get as much information as I can from different sources."

"I was probably the only one in our department that didn't know what she was up to until I overheard her conversation with Rob," I sighed. "Pretty stupid, huh."

He gave me a hug. "Not stupid. You just don't see the evil around you. I'm sorry you have to see it now."

Bonnie had been sheltered all her life. I wondered if she had guessed what Shirley was up to. She'd never said anything about it to me.

"When you overheard that conversation, why didn't you report it?"

Oh, brother, here we go, I thought. He wasn't going to like what I had to say. Rob was going to like it even less. "Rob didn't want it made known. He has a girlfriend. He said she'd be upset. Her father doesn't like him."

"I'll bet she'll be a lot more upset because he gave in." He shook his head. "People need to speak up when they know something illegal is going on." He gave me that look to say I should have gone straight to HR when I overheard the conversation. I didn't want to think about Rob's reaction when Greg got through with him.

"What did Chase have to say?" I decided to change the subject. "Skylar said he called about a break-in at his place.

That's when her body was found."

"She shouldn't have told you anything." I was familiar with that frown. It was the one he always gave me when I asked too many questions.

"She didn't give away any state secrets, Greg. She just told me Chase had called before you left this morning. If there was a break-in at his place, maybe the thief killed her."

"That doesn't explain what she was doing there in the first place? Was she dating anyone?"

I sighed. "I don't have any idea."

"But you've heard the talk." He wasn't going to let me off that easily.

"Okay, I've heard that she recently started dating someone. She never told his name. She was being very secretive about it."

"And," he prompted.

"She bragged that he owned one of the bigger wineries," I finished on a sigh.

"So, that could mean she was dating Chase."

"Now, you're speculating," I accused. "Did the ME find any DNA? What about fingerprints?" I've watched enough CSI and cop shows on television plus listening to Greg talk about his job that I expected there to be a lot of evidence left behind.

"I have to wait for the autopsy, but you know I can't tell you about the evidence, or lack of evidence, we've found. I have to look at everything, including the possibility that Chase was seeing her."

"I don't think Chase would kill anyone, and if you would forget about your past with him, you'd agree. How was she…killed?" My voice faltered on the last word. I knew what Chase's employees told Juan, but I wanted to know what Greg had to say.

He remained silent for so long I figured he was going to ignore my question. He finally gave a weary sigh, shaking his head. "She was strangled. That's up close and personal. She knew her attacker. She'd had sex shortly before she was killed, and placed in the vineyard naked."

He confirmed what Skylar had told me, but I still couldn't keep from gasping. "How could someone do that?" This was the first time he'd given me so much information on one of his cases. I wasn't sure I wanted to know all of it either. Maybe he wanted to shock me so I would stop asking questions.

He patted my hand gently. "Go inside, Pattiann, Mom's waiting for you. I'm not going to release that information to the press, so you can't repeat anything I've told you."

He knew how to ruin a tender moment. I glared at him. "I know enough not to say anything about one of your cases." I headed inside. I didn't like it when he went all official on me. There was a small smile on his lips as I pulled open the screen door. Maybe he was trying to take my mind off how Shirley had been murdered.

Mom was inside waiting for me. She wrapped me in a comforting hug. "Are you all right, Honey? Did you know the woman very well?"

I shook my head. "I'd only worked with her for a few months." I drew a deep breath before asking my question. "Do you think Chase is capable of doing something like this?"

"You never know what drives a person, but I don't want to believe the man we've known would do this." She patted my hand. "Greg will figure it out. It's going to take time."

Time was something Chase might not have, I thought. If someone was trying to frame him, they might get away with it.

~~~

What has that stupid boy gotten himself into now? How could he let something like this happen? This is going to put a bad light on everything I'm doing, everything I've ever done. Pacing around the small room, he tried to come up with a way to spin this so it wasn't what everyone was saying. First thing, he'd have to get a lawyer. *I can't let something like this tarnish my life's work.* It was always about him.

~~~

The next few days seemed to drag as we waited to hear what had happened. Greg was questioning everyone at the hospital who knew Shirley. Rob was furious with me for telling Greg what I'd seen and heard. "I thought you were my friend," he hissed. "Why did you tell him about that? I told you to stay out of it. What if my girlfriend gets wind of this? If she breaks up with me, it will be your fault. I can't let that happen," he muttered.

"I didn't have a choice. Shirley was murdered."

"You always have a choice."

"So did you," I snapped. I was tired of him blaming me for what he did. "You should have reported her instead of giving in."

"You don't know anything. I didn't kill her." He stomped off before I could say anything further.

Much to Joe's disapproval, Chase came over in the evenings hoping to get Greg to tell him something about the investigation. Greg had shut down his winery while they gathered what evidence had been left behind. If anything had been taken, he wasn't saying.

Much like a murder that someone had tried to pin on Skylar last year, Shirley had been killed somewhere else and dumped at Templeton Vineyards. If Greg knew where she had been killed, he wasn't saying.

"I wish he'd tell me what's happening." Chase paced the length of the porch. "I didn't know the woman." I was sure his attorney wouldn't approve of his talking to us about the case. There was no attorney-client privilege with us. If he said something that would incriminate him, he could be nailing his own coffin shut.

"She told several people at the hospital that she had a date with someone from one of the wineries," I said, hoping he'd know something about that.

"Not with me, she didn't. I worked until about seven in the bottling room that night. Then I ordered a pizza. When I finished eating, I cleaned up the leftovers. I don't make a habit of leaving empty bottles and glasses on the porch. That just invites wild animals to come around. Everyone knows that." He threw himself into one of the wicker chairs on the porch in front of Mom and Joe's place.

Bonnie and I had been going out to the winery after work, hoping to learn something new. Everything Chase said was a rehash of what he'd told Greg and us before. Bonnie vacillated between believing him innocent one minute and guilty the next.

When Ty's big truck pulled into the lane my heart rate soared. Because of our crazy schedules we didn't get to see each other as often as I'd like. The flu epidemic was easing, and he wasn't coming into the hospital as often now.

"I figured this is where you'd be when you weren't at home." His smile lit up his face, turning me to mush. Sitting down on the porch step closest to me, he took my hand in his much bigger one.

Mom stepped out, giving him a smile. "Hello, Ty. Can I get you something to drink?" We all had frosted glasses of lemonade or iced tea. She was the consummate hostess, not wanting anyone to do without.

"Iced tea would be great, Mrs. Barnes. Thank you."

"Oh, now, none of that stuff. It's Dora. We're all friends here." Joe snorted when she included Chase in that statement. She frowned down at him, giving his shoulder a pat. He would never consider Chase a friend.

A few minutes later, Greg and Skylar joined us, offering everyone a glass of wine. Bonnie was riding with me, so she accepted, but I was satisfied with my lemonade. Greg gave Chase a sharp look, but didn't say anything. I wasn't sure if he still considered Chase a person of interest, or he just didn't like him.

Chase glared at Greg. He looked like he was ready for a fight. "How stupid do you think I am to put the body of a woman I had killed on my own property?"

A smirk curled Greg's lips. "I don't think you want me to

answer that question. It might not be as stupid as you suggest. It is rather diabolical though, figuring no one would think you'd do something that dumb. It's sort of like reverse psychology."

"I don't care what kind of psychology you call it. I didn't kill that woman. If you don't have anything on me, when are you going to clear my place so I can get back to work?" His legs were braced apart, and his fists rested on his hips. "I can't close down my tasting room over the weekend. I also have work that I need to do. What's taking you so long?" Animosity came off him in waves.

For a long moment, I thought Greg was going to ignore him. Finally he nodded his head. "My guys can take down the crime scene tape in the morning."

"Does that mean you know who killed Shirley?" Bonnie asked hopefully.

"Not yet."

"It wasn't me," Chase stated emphatically.

Greg let the silence draw out again before giving another nod. "Probably not, but you don't have an alibi."

"I also don't have a motive. I didn't know the woman."

"She came in the tasting room," Bonnie said softly.

"What?" Greg and Chase spoke at the same time. Greg shot him a dirty look before turning to Bonnie. "When was that?"

She shrugged, suddenly shy when all eyes turned on her. "I don't know, sometime that first weekend I worked there. It was busy. I just remember being surprised to see her there. She was never very sociable at work."

"Did you talk to her?" Greg's voice was sharp and intimidating, causing Bonnie to cower. Skylar nudged him, and he softened his voice. "Who waited on her?"

"I tried, but she ignored me. She only had eyes for Chase. She waited until he was free." She gave him an apologetic look. "If there's a good-looking man in the room, any woman might as well be invisible."

It surprised me that Bonnie was aware of Shirley's actions while I'd overlooked what should have been obvious. Until I overheard her conversation with Rob, I hadn't been aware of what she had been up to. I guess I was the naïve one instead of Bonnie.

Greg turned to Chase. "So you did know her." He growled the accusation. "Did she try to put the make on you?"

"So now you think I killed her because she flirted with me? Or maybe she rejected my advances, and I killed her for that. You're really stretching here, Wilkinson." He sneered at Greg. He wasn't doing himself a favor by antagonizing Greg.

Letting the silence draw out, Greg didn't say anything. "Do you know how many people go through the tasting room on any given weekend?" Chase finally asked into the silence. "I try to talk to as many people as possible. I can't be expected to remember everyone that comes in, or what I said to them. I certainly don't remember anyone hitting on me. That would have stuck in my memory. I don't make a habit of accepting offers of sex from women I don't know either." Was he aware of what she'd been doing at the hospital?

"You get a lot of offers like that?" Greg lifted one eyebrow in question.

Chase's face turned red, but he didn't back down. "I've had a couple. I'm sure Skylar has had a few as well." All eyes turned to Skylar, and she lifted one shoulder in a shrug. From the look on Greg's face, that must mean yes. I'm sure he'd bring it up later when they were alone.

"After being at several tasting rooms, people get a little tipsy," Chase said. "Somctimes the women will flirt with me. If a woman is working behind the bar, the men flirt with her. I noticed several men flirting with Bonnie last weekend, too." He looked at her, and she nodded. Her face was pink now.

Turning away from Chase, Greg looked at Bonnie. "Did she buy anything?"

She nodded. "She bought three bottles."

"If you found my fingerprints on the bottle, that would be

why," Chase said. "I handle every bottle that goes out my door. Did you find fingerprints on the glasses? Were they from my winery?"

Once again, I thought Greg was going to ignore the questions. Finally he gave a frustrated sigh. "Neither glass had your logo. One of the glasses had her fingerprints. The prints on the other one were smudged, nothing that could be used. It seems that the rim and inside of the glass was washed to remove any DNA." That seemed deliberate to leave behind something, but nothing that would identify the user.

Chase shook his head at that. "I must be the most clever criminal, or the dumbest, to do all that, and still leave her where she could be found on my own property. Why would someone wash the glass, but leave smudged prints on it?" Greg didn't have an answer for that. "What did my security cameras show?" His winery was almost as secure as Fort Knox with cameras on every building including his house.

"Well, you see, that's another problem. Someone managed to avoid them, probably someone who knew where they were. The last person caught on camera is the pizza delivery guy bringing your dinner. So who put the glasses and wine bottle on the table?" Greg was yanking his chain because he didn't like him.

"It wasn't me." Chase was getting more agitated by the minute.

"You got many enemies around here?" He'd probably asked these questions when Shirley's body was first discovered.

Chase sighed. "Not around here I don't." He stood up. "I don't need this. I've answered all your questions several times. Someone puts a dead woman in my vineyard, and you treat me like a suspect. Do your damn job, and find out who did this."

Was I the only one to pick up on Chase's comment about no enemies around here? I wondered what his father would do if he heard about the trouble his son was in. Would he help him, or leave him to twist in the wind?

"If you don't like the company, you shouldn't come over," Greg said.

"That's enough, Greg." Mom caught the last of this exchange as she brought out Ty's iced tea. "Chase, you don't have to leave. Greg will behave himself." Her glare could intimidate anyone, including my brother.

"Thanks, Dora, but maybe I can get a little work done tonight. I'm way behind on everything." He shot Greg a malicious look before heading for his truck.

When the big truck pulled out of the lane I mentally compared it to the one that had followed me several days ago. George's vague comment that the person following me was 'sort of' the guy I was with at the diner still puzzled me. I had no idea what he meant.

"You don't really think he killed her, do you?" Bonnie asked into the silence that had stretched out after Chase left.

Greg answered with a shrug.

CHAPTER TWELVE

Shirley's murder was still the hot topic in the hospital, and the town. Greg still had no suspects. Whoever killed her had left nothing behind. He would like to have charged Chase with something, but there was no evidence that he'd been involved with her.

Rob was still angry at me after Greg questioned him a second time. He'd been in class that evening, but got out early enough that he could have stopped by Shirley's apartment. His anger seemed a little over the top. There had to be something else going on with him.

"You just had to stick your nose where it didn't belong," Rob hissed at me. "This is all your fault."

"What are you talking about now?" Greg hadn't charged him with anything, so what was his problem?

"Jill broke up with me."

I gasped. "Why would she do that?" I reached out to touch his arm, but he pulled away.

"She said she couldn't trust me. If you'd kept your mouth shut like I asked you to, she never would have known about this."

"Of course she would have," I argued. "What Shirley was doing here has been in the paper."

"That's just it. If you hadn't said anything about what she was doing, it wouldn't have been in the paper."

"Rob, someone killed her."

"Well, it wasn't me."

"I know that, but if what she was doing is what got her killed, Greg needed to know." I'd explained this to him before, but it hadn't done any good.

"Why did she break up with you? This wasn't your fault. That's like blaming the victim after she's been raped."

"You try telling her that," he snapped. "On second thought, don't tell her anything. I don't want you anywhere near her. You've done enough damage."

"I'm sorry she broke up with you, but that isn't my fault."

"Right. Keep telling yourself that. Maybe you'll believe it someday. Jill never would have found out any of this if you had kept your mouth shut."

"So you're saying what she didn't know wouldn't hurt you. Is that it?" He glared at me, but ignored my question.

"Just stay away from me, and keep your mouth shut or you'll be sorry." My stomach churned at his barely veiled threat. He sounded more angry than heartbroken over the breakup. Was something else going on that I didn't understand? Didn't he realize I had no choice but to tell Greg what I knew? If I'd been in Jill's place, I wasn't sure how I would handle the same situation. I'd like to think I'd blame the person doing the harassing, not the victim.

That night, instead of a long scratch on the side of my car, the driver's side window had been broken out. There was glass over the front seat and on the parking lot. My Louisville Slugger was missing. I suspected Rob had done this, but again I had no proof.

"Who would do this?" Bonnie asked as we waited for Security to come out to take pictures of the damage.

When Sam rolled up in his golf cart, he shook his head. "It looks like you've gotten on someone's bad side, Pattiann. Got any ideas who that would be?" He raised his eyebrows in question.

"You wouldn't be able to help me with that, would you?" I avoided answering his question. "The last time the security cameras weren't any help."

"I'll take another look, but don't hold your breath. Everyone working here knows where the cameras are. Anyone out for mischief knows what to look for so they can avoid them." He shook his head. "I brought out the shop vac to pick up this glass."

If this continued, my insurance rate would go up. I didn't want that to happen, but I didn't know how to stop whoever was doing this. Confronting Rob didn't sound like a wise move. He already hated me.

Greg was home when Bonnie and I arrived a short time later. We'd stopped to pick up dinner on the way out of town. Manuel's Mexican Restaurant had excellent take-out. Since we were there almost weekly, they knew what each of us wanted without even asking.

"What took you so long?" he teased. "I was about to eat some of Cody's food." Hearing his name, Cody stood up to see if I had something for him.

"Sorry, boy." I held the box out of his reach so he couldn't get a taste. He was usually good about leaving table food alone, but the customers spoiled him. "I don't think you'd like what we have." I laughed when he sniffed the air, licking his chops. I wasn't going to give him a chance to try what we had though. If he got one lick, he might want another.

"What happened to your window?" Greg frowned at me. I had hoped he wouldn't notice, but no such luck.

Ty pulled into the lane then, distracting him from any more questions. I had called him while I waited for Sam to finish vacuuming up the glass to see if he wanted to join us. "It looks like my baby sister is serious for a change." Greg wrapped his arm around my neck, pulling me close. "I approve," he whispered, placing a kiss in my hair. "Even if he is a fireman." He chuckled when I poked him in the ribs.

Bonnie headed for the porch to help Mom finish setting the wicker patio table. There were chairs enough for everyone. This was getting to be a nightly gathering. We all wanted to find out the latest on the murder.

Ty placed a kiss on my lips, not my hair, pulling me close to his side with one arm while taking the box out of my hands with the other. "What happened to your window?"

"Yeah," Greg said. "You didn't answer me." His forehead creased with his frown.

"Vandals in the parking lot at the hospital, I guess." I shrugged, trying to make light of what happened. I headed for the porch. "Let's eat before everything gets cold."

"This is the second time your car has been vandalized. Don't they have Security out there?" Greg wasn't going to let the subject drop.

"The guard said he'd check the cameras tonight. I don't hold out much hope. I'll be parking right where the cameras are from now on. Is there anything new on the investigation?" It was an obvious attempt to change the subject.

"The forensic team went through her apartment with a fine-toothed comb," Greg said. "There were several bottles of wine from different wineries in the area, including Templeton Vineyards. Nothing incriminating there," he said on a sigh.

"There was no sign that she'd had a visitor that night either. It looked like a cleaning crew had swept through there." He stopped to take a bite out of his burrito. "There were fresh sheets on the bed, and sheets in the washing machine. If there had been any evidence on them, it went down the drain. I'm still talking to the men at the hospital, but so far no one admits to being upset enough to kill her." With the exception of Rob, I thought. He was ready to do me in, not just Shirley.

"A couple of our guys went out with her," Ty said. "But she wasn't interested in the dating scene. It was more of a power game with her. When she didn't have anything she could hold over their heads, she lost interest. That didn't stop her from flirting though. She flirted with anything in long pants." He lifted his broad shoulders in a shrug. "There was no way I was going to get caught up in that sort of game."

"Was she killed because of what she was doing?" Bonnie asked softly. "Or was there another reason? She hadn't lived here very long, and didn't know a lot of people." Her voice quivered. Her rather restrictive life hadn't prepared her for something like murder. But who's had?

Greg cleared his throat, but remained silent for a long moment. It meant he knew something, but was trying to decide whether to say anything. "We don't have a clear motive yet. Men aren't the only ones who think they can get away with that sort of thing. Some of the other nurses wanted her job, but not bad enough to kill her. Other than that and sexually harassing some of the men at the hospital, we haven't found anyone here with a motive," he finally said.

"No one here," Joe said. "Does that mean there is someone somewhere else with a possible motive?"

"Yeah," Greg reluctantly admitted. "We contacted her former employer. She had pulled the same stunt there." He paused. "She was given the choice of resigning with nothing in her employee record, or being fired with charges filed against her."

"Why wouldn't they file charges against her?" Mom asked. "Sexual harassment is against the law."

"Yeah, but most employers don't want that kind of publicity or the hassle of a lawsuit. It's easier to sweep it under the proverbial rug. As long as she resigned, and they could pay off her victims, they were fine."

"But there's more," Joe said. "Right?" He was very good at reading Greg's non-verbal signs.

Reluctantly, Greg nodded his head. "It wasn't until after she left when they discovered that sexual harassment wasn't the only thing she was up to." He had captured our attention now. "While she was having her fun with the men, she was also switching out some of the meds the patients were given. Maybe the harassment was a smoke screen for the theft." He shrugged. "We'll never know for sure.

"She was stealing drugs from the patients?" Bonnie and I spoke at the same time.

Greg nodded. "She was, or she had an accomplice."

"Was she selling the drugs?" I asked. How could she get away with that?

"Her former employer hasn't been very forthcoming on the issue. They just want it to go away."

"Did anyone die because she switched their meds?" The thought was so horrifying I could barely get the words out.

How could a trained nurse do something like that?

Greg shrugged. "Like I said, the hospital isn't talking."

"Do you think someone from that hospital came here and killed her?" Mom asked. "If one of her patients died because of what she did, maybe a relative came here to get even." Revenge was a good motive for murder. We'd found that out a year ago.

"That's a good theory, but that's all it is right now. Until we can get more information from the hospital, we can't even say for sure that she was the one stealing the drugs. It could have been a totally unrelated crime." It didn't sound like he believed that.

"We'll figure it out, but it's going to take time. If the hospital in Portland had turned her in for harassment, she might still be alive. In jail, but alive," he said with a sigh.

"She was from Portland, Oregon?" That surprised me. Chase's father owned a company there. Did she know who Chase's family is? I didn't know if that had anything to do with her death either.

"Does that mean something to you?" Greg frowned at me.

"No, I just didn't know where she was from." How well known was the Templeton name in Oregon? Did that have anything to do with her murder? It might be an interesting fact to follow up on.

"Has anyone heard anything more from either the realtor or lawyer again?" I changed the subject. We had been concentrating on the murder, and forgot all about them. I wasn't sure if they had anything to do with Shirley's murder though. There didn't seem to be any connection. What they had been doing wasn't illegal, so Greg wasn't investigating them.

All eyes turned to Skylar, and she shook her head. "Maybe they finally got the message that no one wanted to sell their businesses."

"I checked out the lawyer," Greg put in. "He's out of Phoenix. He usually skirts the line between legal and illegal.

He's one of those attorneys that give the law profession a bad name."

Ty finished his iced tea, setting down the glass. "I hate to call it a night, but I'm on shift early tomorrow. Thanks for inviting me to dinner." He stood up.

"I'll walk you out." He had parked beside my car on the other side of the tasting room. Lacing his long fingers through mine, he pulled me close for a kiss in the dark. He'd be on shift for the next forty-eight hours. That meant the only time I would see him was if he brought a patient to the hospital. The crazy hours we both kept made it difficult to find out if we could have a lasting relationship. But I figured he was worth the time and effort it was going to take to figure it out.

He leaned against the side of his truck, pulling me in for another kiss. "I'll call you when I can. Maybe we can go for dinner the next time I'm off."

"I'd like that." For several minutes there was no need for words. Greg was right, I'd finally found a guy I could get serious about.

When he lifted his head, he had to clear his throat before he could make his voice work. "I'd better get going. I need to get some sleep tonight." With a final kiss that rocked me to my toes and made them curl, he got in his truck. "I'll call you when I can. Be careful."

I watched as the taillights of his truck disappeared in the dark before going back to the porch. Did he really think someone was stalking me? I was still keeping that possibility to myself. Greg had enough to do without my adding to it. There hadn't been any more sightings of someone following me, so maybe we'd been wrong.

Bonnie and I headed home a few minutes later. We needed to get some sleep as well. Going past Templeton Vineyards, I slowed down. Once again, Chase was sitting on the porch. Bonnie looked out the window at him. "He looks so lonely," she said quietly. "I feel sorry for him. He doesn't have many friends."

I nodded my head in agreement. He hadn't had a happy life before moving here. His father had been a tyrant, demanding total obedience. When Chase rebelled, he had been cut off from his family. He had kept to himself after moving to New Haven. Bonnie's family had kept her separated from any friends, but at least they loved her.

~~~

The hospital was still reeling from the news of Shirley's activities and her murder. As head nurse in the Emergency Department, she didn't have the opportunity to switch meds given to the patients. But an audit was being made just in case. Since her activities had been made public, the hospital couldn't deny what had been going on. They were interviewing anyone she came in contact with, not just the ER staff. I supposed Rob would blame me for that as well.

Several other men had admitted Shirley had pressured them to have sex with her. They were young, mostly working their first jobs. She had promised to help them with their careers. If they didn't go along with her demands, she threatened to get them fired.

The hospital had offered counseling to anyone she had been involved with. I didn't know if anyone took them up on the offer. Mostly they were embarrassed. Rob was the only one angry enough to threaten me for telling what I knew. Maybe he had more to lose.

"She'd been a very busy woman in the short time she'd worked at the hospital," Bonnie said. "Why didn't anyone report what she was doing? Did they really believe she had enough power to get them fired?"

Those were questions I wanted to ask Linda in HR. I wasn't surprised when she stopped at the nurses' station the next day. It was my turn to have this little chat. "If you're not busy, could we go somewhere to talk?" Giving a sigh, I followed her to the break room.

"Did you know what Shirley was doing?" I turned the tables on her, asking the question before she could ask me.
~~~

"I had heard the rumors, but I had no direct knowledge about who was involved," she admitted. She was being careful to cover her own behind.

"I couldn't do anything based on rumors alone. No one came to me with a complaint. I didn't have any names just that it was going on. I kept hoping someone would come forward." She drew a deep breath. "There are always cases where doctors and nurses hook up using empty patient rooms. But that's usually by mutual consent."

"But this was different," I said. "She was threatening the men if they didn't agree to her demands."

"I didn't know she was involved until days before she was killed. Did you know what was going on?" She turned my question back on me. It was my turn to sigh.

"Not until recently," I admitted.

"Yet you didn't say anything either. I was hoping that was why you had come to see me. What was that all about?"

"Like I told you, I wanted to make sure it wasn't against hospital policy for me to help out in my sister-in-law's winery." I couldn't look her in the face now.

"You'd been working there for over a year. Why the sudden need to check it out?"

"Okay," I sighed. "Shirley made a veiled threat after…"

"Yes?" She prompted when I didn't finish the sentence. My face grew hot as I explained about seeing her and Rob leaving an empty room together. "Why didn't you tell me about that? About either incident? I could have stopped her."

"Rob kept telling me not to say anything. He was afraid of losing his job. He wanted a nursing position here after he graduated. She'd promised to put in a good word for him."

She shook her head. "Her word wouldn't have meant anything if he had come to me in the first place." She gave a frustrated sigh. "This is how predators get away with their crimes for so long. The victims are too afraid to say anything. I don't know what she could have been holding over anyone's head to make them agree."

"Just the threat of losing their job would do it," I said. At least that's what Rob claimed. If he'd gone to Linda when it first started, his girlfriend wouldn't have broken up with him. I wasn't sure if he would get the nursing job now.

"Did Rob threaten you to keep you quiet?" She tilted her head to one side.

"Not in so many words," I admitted.

"But you got his point."

I nodded. "Why didn't the hospital in Oregon report what she'd been doing there?" I wanted to change the subject. I still didn't understand why employers let things like this slide. "If it had been on her record, she wouldn't have been hired here." At least I hoped they wouldn't have hired her, I silently added.

"Like most employers, they were afraid of a lawsuit." She shrugged. In my estimation, letting someone get away with a crime because you were afraid of a lawsuit was a cop-out.

"Did you know about missing and misdirected drugs at the last place she worked?" I knew the hospital was doing an audit on all drugs. Even though Shirley didn't have the same access to drugs in the ER as she would on a regular patient floor, she still had access to drugs.

Linda shook her head. "Not until after she was killed. I wish the Portland hospital had said something about that when her references were checked. Your brother is the one who informed me about that." There was little left to be said, and I stood up.

"Maybe I should have said more when I came to see you, but I was trying to keep Rob's name out of it. He wasn't the one that threatened me."

"Not that time, but he did later." Her expression held reproach. If I had told her the whole story at that time, would Shirley still be alive? Did her murder have anything to do with what she was doing at the hospital? Or was there another motive?

I would always have to carry that around with me. Greg was still looking for the motive for her murder. There was no mention of missing drugs at our hospital. I wasn't sure Linda would admit it if there was. The hospital was still trying to cover their collective backsides.

Rob was lurking around outside the break room when I walked out a few minutes later. "Haven't you done enough damage?" he snarled.

"What exactly did I do to you?"

"You ruined everything, that's what. I had things all planned out with Jill. That's all gone to hell now because you just had to tell everything you know."

"There are a few things I didn't tell," I countered. "Like how someone keyed the side of my car. Or about the window of my car that someone busted out. You wouldn't happen to know anything about either of those things, would you?"

"It sounds to me like someone was getting a little payback." His lips curled in a smirk.

"Is that a confession, Rob?" Neither of us had noticed Linda standing the doorway of the break room. "Maybe I should have a word with you next. Shall we take this to my office?" She held out her arm, pointing down the hall.

"No, I don't have anything to say. Just leave me alone." He pushed his way past me, knocking me into the wall.

"We will have this talk, Rob," she called out to his retreating form. She turned to me with concern in her eyes. "Are you all right?"

"I'm fine." I rubbed my shoulder where it had connected with the wall.

"Did you report the damage to your car to Security?"

I nodded my head. "Nothing showed up on the security tapes. I'm parking next to one of those cameras now."

"Be careful, Pattiann. He sounds angry enough to do something very foolish. I'm here if there's anything I can do for you." She walked off, shaking her head.

Something was going on with Rob. He had been too relieved that Shirley was gone, and too insistent that I remain silent about his involvement with her. He couldn't be blamed for giving in to Shirley's demands if he really feared he would lose his job. It sounded like he had something planned with Jill, more than he'd let on.

I didn't know what kind of car he drove, but I was going to find out. If he drove a pickup, he could be the one following me instead of Chase. He was probably more dangerous as well.

CHAPTER THIRTEEN

Martha had been offered the job as head nurse in the Emergency Department after Shirley's murder. She jumped at the opportunity, and strutted around like a proud peacock. She had been giving Bonnie and me some grief about us being roommates. There was nothing in the employee handbook against it, but she wanted to throw her weight around.

She went so far as to threaten to transfer one of us to a different shift, or maybe a different department. "It isn't a good policy to have people who are living together also working together," she had announced only days after taking over the new position. It would almost be worth transferring to get away from her.

She had finally relented, at least for now, allowing Bonnie and me to remain on the same shift. She was right about one thing though; living and working together might be too much of a good thing. We each needed our own space. Neither of us wanted to ruin our friendship with too much togetherness.

Bonnie bounced out of bed in the morning ready for the day to begin, while it took a little longer for me to get going. Leaving for work at separate times would allow us to have a few minutes of alone time before the day started. Taking our own cars to work would also give us the opportunity to do something after work if we wanted.

Since we were still going to the winery each day to find out if Greg had anything new on the murder, having only one car was more practical. We'd have to figure it out when this mystery was solved.

"Chase was waiting for me when I came back from lunch," Bonnie whispered. The bag of fast food in her hand was all but forgotten. "He wanted to know if I'd have dinner with him tonight. He was being all mysterious."

"Do you want to go out with him again?"

She thought about that for a minute. "Yeah, I guess, but

I'm going out with Walt, too. I shouldn't be dating two guys at the same time, should I?" This was all new territory for her. "It's not like I'm going steady with either of them, but if I have to choose, I'd rather go out with Walt."

"What did you tell Chase?"

"I didn't want to hurt his feelings, so I said yes." Sometimes she was too nice for her own good. She didn't want to hurt anyone's feelings, which allowed them to take advantage of her. "He came all the way to town to ask me. I don't know why he didn't just call me. I gave him my phone number when I started working for him. Maybe I should have told him I'm seeing someone else." She dipped into the bag for a French fry. "You don't think he's dangerous, do you?" Greg still hadn't arrested anyone for Shirley's murder.

"No, I don't think he's dangerous. How was he over the weekend?" She'd been working in his tasting room just a few days ago. If he wanted to ask her out, why hadn't he asked her then? After the commotion over Shirley's murder, he had a lot on his mind. Maybe he just forgot, I told myself.

"I didn't think he went out much," she added. "But he's been in town several times lately." I had to agree with her on that point. He had been stepping out of his comfort zone a lot lately. Maybe he was finally trying to make friends.

The door swished open admitting a young couple holding a crying baby. That was all the time we had to think about her dilemma. Something odd was going on with Chase though.

Instead of going to the winery after work, I decided to spend a quiet evening at home while Bonnie went to dinner with Chase. She was spending as many nights at my place as she was at her apartment. It was only a matter of days before she moved in full time. It was still early when I heard his big pickup pull into the drive. She had to be at the hospital early in the morning, so that probably accounted for the early night.

It was only a few minutes before I heard her key in the lock, and the truck drive away. He hadn't even walked her to the door. That didn't bode well for how the evening went. She looked sad when she stepped inside.

"What happened? Didn't you have a good time?" I set aside the book I'd been reading.

"Well, he sort of got romantic." She shook her head like she couldn't believe he did that.

"Did he try something with you? Are you okay?" I was off the couch in an instant. I didn't want to believe he would try to force himself on her. If he did, I wouldn't let it go. I'd learned my lesson on that score.

She shook her head. "No, it wasn't like that. He was sort of…." She paused, trying to find the right word. "Mushy," she finished her sentence giving a small shudder. I coughed to cover up the laugh that threatened to spill over. Apparently she wasn't ready for mushy romance.

"Tell me what happened." I took her hand leading her to the couch where she plopped down beside me.

Drawing a deep breath, she let it out on a sigh. "He said he really liked me, and wanted to keep dating me. He kissed the back of my hand like I've seen them do in movies. It was kind of embarrassing right there in the restaurant." She gave a bigger shudder this time, as unshed tears sparkled in her brown eyes.

"He said it wouldn't be right if I continued working for him since he was feeling that way." She looked at me, as a fat tear slid down her cheek. "I guess he fired me. He made it sound like this is a big love affair, or something. I thought we were just having fun being friends."

"What did you tell him?"

"I said I wanted to keep working for him. I don't see any reason I can't work for him and still go out with him." She'd been staring at her hands, but now looked up at me. "I'd rather work for him than date him." She sniffed. "I liked working in the tasting room."

"Did you tell him that?" That would cool down his romantic ideas in a hurry. I didn't bother to cover my smile this time. It was his business, and he could make up his own rules. But I saw no reason she couldn't date him, and work for him at the same time. This was another instance where he was acting strange.

She shook her head. "No," she said sadly. "I guess he got the message though. He brought me right home as soon as we finished eating."

"Are you still going to work for him? Did he say anything about that?"

She shook her head again. "Even if we aren't dating, I can't keep working for him now. That would really be awkward. Do you think any of the other wineries need someone to help out?" Staying home on her four days off was like punishment to her.

"Don't worry about it tonight. We'll figure something out. We'll check with Skylar tomorrow. She'll know if anyone could use a little help. Until then you can come with me. I know she won't mind." Chase had hurt her, whether intentionally or not. I didn't know what was wrong with him. Why would he think it made any difference if they were dating?

~~~

"What the devil are you doing here?" The older man stared at a younger version of himself.

Without waiting for an invitation, he pushed his way into the room. "I was wondering the same thing about you. What are you doing here? You've never shown any interest in anything unless it directly affects you."

"What I do is none of your business." He grabbed at the younger man's arm, attempting to keep him from going any further.

"Well, see, that's where you're wrong, it is my business." He brushed off the hand gripping his arm to wander around the room. Stopping at the desk, he examined the papers there, looking up at the older man. "You seem to be working in opposition to me." He lifted up the stack of papers. "What were your plans? Did you suddenly grow a conscience? Do
~~~

you really think it will make a difference?"

The older man pushed him away from the small table, grabbing at the papers. "This is my business. It's time for you to leave."

"No, I think it's time for you to leave. Permanently." Without giving the man the chance to answer, his hand shot out, slashing the older man across the neck.

Grabbing his neck, his eyes bulged out. His mouth worked, trying to form a word, or a scream, but nothing came out. He collapsed silently to the floor.

"I did it," he muttered, although there was no one to hear him now. "I really did it." He felt pumped, the blood in his veins sang with energy. Or maybe it was the adrenalin, but it didn't really matter. He was finally rid of the tyrant. He hadn't been sure he could do it. He dropped the sharp knife in the quickly growing pool of blood on the floor.

There was blood everywhere, including on him. This time he'd come prepared. Stripping off the bloody latex gloves, he picked up the bag he'd brought with him. He made sure his fingerprints wouldn't be on the knife. He dispensed with the bloody polo shirt he'd been wearing when he came in, tossing it in the bag along with the gloves.

Using another pair of gloves, he went through the papers on the desk. They confirmed his suspicions. He was trying to buy the wineries. He'd even succeeded on getting one of them. It surprised him to see the contracts for the empty parcels the old man had been planning on buying. Everything was in the company name.

For several minutes he debated whether to take them, or leave them behind. Everyone knew someone was trying to buy up the wineries in the area. Leaving them was further proof of that. This might even work in his favor. It would provide a motive. He chuckled at that.

The old man's wallet was on the desk. There was a fake driver's license along with a credit card matching the name on the license. Who knew the old man was so inventive? The real license and credit card were in with a wad of cash. Leaving the cash, he put the license and credit card where the fake ones had been.

Being careful not to step in the pool of blood, he changed into a fresh set of clothes right down to the shoes. He listened at the door for any sounds. When he was confident there was no one in the corridor, he opened the door using a hanky so he wouldn't leave any fingerprints there either. The scene was set, let's see what the sheriff does with it.

There were several people in the lobby as he passed through, but they didn't pay any attention to him. A fake beard and a hat pulled low over his forehead was the only disguise he needed. No one would connect him to the clean-shaven man that came through a short time ago.

~~~

It was after lunch when the ambulance pulled into the emergency bay. They hadn't bothered with the sirens. That meant the patient wasn't critical, or it was too late for him or her.

"Are you all right?" I whispered. Ty's face was ashen as he pulled the gurney out of the back of the ambulance. A muscle jumped in his jaw.

He shook his head. "No, I'm not. This is a gruesome one." I walked beside him as he maneuvered the gurney to the side door. The body bag told me this patient was beyond needing our help.

"An accident?" I asked, hoping whatever happened wasn't connected to the other things that had been going on.

He shook his head, but didn't say anything as he pushed the gurney to the service elevator going down to the morgue in the hospital basement.

I didn't see him when he came back a short time later, so I had no idea who had died or how. If Ty said it was gruesome, it had to be pretty bad.

A hospital is like a small town within a small town. Gossip travels fast. We quickly learned there had been another
~~~

murder, this time at the only hotel in New Haven. The name of the victim was being withheld until the next of kin could be notified. I was anxious for the day to end so I could head out to Sky Vineyards. Maybe Greg would be willing to share some of the details with us.

"You arrested Chase?" I couldn't believe Greg would do that. "Why?" That wasn't the kind of details I had been hoping for. We were all gathered on the porch in front of Mom and Joe's side of the house.

"Pattiann, I don't have to account to you for my actions. I know what I'm doing. Besides, I didn't arrest him." He sighed like he wished he had. Something about this case had him tied up in a knot. "I just brought him in for questioning. I wouldn't be doing my job if I didn't question him."

"What does Chase have to do with the murder in town?" Bonnie asked the question this time.

"He was seen entering the hotel lobby around the time of death. There was also evidence found at the scene that implicated him, and…" He paused.

"And?" We all asked at the same time. All except Ty, he was being unusually quiet.

"And the victim was his father," Greg finished on a sigh.

I gasped. "What was he doing here? They haven't spoken to each other in years." The words were out before I could stop them.

"You know this how?" Greg lifted his brow in question.

I squirmed in my chair. I should have kept my mouth shut, but it was too late for that. There was no way I could avoid telling about having dinner with Chase now. Greg wasn't going to be happy that I'd kept that fact to myself. I didn't see that it had anything to do with either murder though.

"I thought the man was killed sometime early last night." Bonnie asked the question before Greg could question me further.

"Yes, that's right. The ME said the victim was killed between nine and nine-thirty. His body was found this morning when the maid came in to clean the room. The desk clerk at the hotel and several guests claim to have seen Chase walking through the lobby around that time."

Bonnie frowned, shaking her head. "It couldn't have been him. He was at his place when we left here last night. That was nine-fifteen." She looked at me for confirmation. When I nodded, she continued. "He couldn't have been in both places at the same time." It had been two days since Bonnie had dinner with Chase. She managed to look past her hurt, and stick up for him.

"She's right. Chase was sitting on the front porch at his place when we drove past. Either those people were wrong about the time, or it wasn't Chase."

"Are you sure it was Chase sitting there? It was dark when you left, and his house is a little way from the road."

"Not that far. Besides, who else would be there at that time of night? He lives alone."

"I'm just saying you couldn't see him clearly from the road. He's had men working security for him in the past. Maybe he has them again since the body was found in his vineyard."

"And Chase told them they could sit on the porch, and have a glass of wine while he goes into town to kill someone? Is that what you're thinking? I didn't realize Chase was that diabolical?" I didn't know why I was defending him after the way he had treated Bonnie.

"That's not what I said," Greg snapped. He was getting defensive. I'd never questioned him before on any of his cases. I'd never known one of his suspects either. That made a big difference.

"That's what it sounds like. If I didn't know better, I'd say you want Chase to be guilty simply because you don't like him." The instant the words were out, I knew I was wrong. Greg would never do that. I didn't want to back down though.

"That's enough, young lady. Sit down. You both need to calm down and apologize to each other." Mom hadn't said anything until right then. I thought about defying her order, but decided against it. I sat down again.

Bonnie's eyes were as big as saucers, and tears shimmered in them now. "I'm sorry," she whispered. "I didn't mean to cause a fight." One big tear slipped down her cheek. "I just thought Greg should know Chase was home when we left here last night." Being an only child, she had no experience with the fights siblings could get into.

"This isn't your fault, Bonnie." Mom patted her arm comfortingly. "The blame falls on these two." She gave each of us what I had always called the 'stink eye' when we were growing up. It was enough to bring even the most rebellious child into submission. It had the same effect now.

"I'm sorry, Bonnie." I looked at Greg. "I didn't mean that last part," I added grudgingly. As apologies go, it was a half-hearted at best. He was being just as pigheaded as I was. "But she's right. Chase was home at nine-fifteen when we drove past his place. He couldn't have been in town. Someone is mistaken, and it isn't us," I added stubbornly, daring him to argue this time.

"Are you sure about the time you left last night?" His tone was mild now. I was still waiting for him to apologize, if not to me, to Bonnie.

When Mom nudged him with her foot, he sighed, looking down at his hands for a moment. "I'm sorry, both of you. You have to understand that I know what I'm doing. I'm not going to arrest someone simply because I don't like them." His gaze shifted to me at that. "I wouldn't plant evidence either."

"I know that. I said I was sorry." Even I could hear the petulant tone in my voice.

"Not really," he laughed, easing the tension. "But I'll take what I can get." He paused for a moment, thinking about what he was going to say next. "At least three people swear they saw Chase enter the lobby between eight-forty-five and nine o'clock. They could be wrong about the time, but the ME is certain about the time of death."

"Why are they so positive it was Chase?" Skylar asked the question this time. "If they were tourists, how could they be certain it was him? Chase isn't all that active in the town. It would be interesting to know how they could identify him."

Greg frowned, thinking that over. "One of my deputies questioned them. I'll have to find out how they could give a positive identification."

"What was Chase's father doing in town?" That still struck me as odd after what Chase had said about his relationship with the man.

"Why wouldn't he be here, Honey?" Mom asked. "He probably came to see his son."

"Chase hasn't talked to anyone in his family in years." I said, drawing a deep breath. I might as well get it all out there. I didn't want Chase to be accused of murder if he didn't do it.

"How do you know that?" Greg's dark gaze turned to me.

"A couple of weeks ago I stopped at the Roadside Café when I left work to get something to eat. Chase was there. He asked me to join him."

Greg's brows lowered over his eyes. "And he told you all about his family troubles?" I shrugged, but didn't say anything. "You didn't think to mention it until now?"

"It never came up in conversation. Besides, I knew how you would react. I didn't see any harm in it. All we did was talk and have dinner. It was no big deal. It didn't have anything to do with Shirley's murder, or this one." I glanced at Ty. I didn't want him to think I was dating Chase, and stop seeing me.

"What did he say about his family?" Mom spoke up before we could get in another argument.

"His father owns a business in Portland."

Before I could continue, Greg interrupted. "He's from Portland? You didn't think to mention that fact when Shirley was murdered?"

"Just because they were both from the same city doesn't mean they knew each other. It's a big place. He hasn't lived there for a long time."

"All right, go on. What else did he say about his father?" Greg still wasn't happy with me, but he let me talk.

"He's sort of a big shot in Oregon. He expected his son to follow in his footsteps, but Chase had other ideas. He wanted to be a vintner. His father didn't approve. Chase left home right after high school to study in Australia for several years before coming here to open his winery. They haven't spoken since."

"The fact that Shirley and Chase were both from Portland seems quite a coincidence," Greg stated. "I don't believe in coincidences in police work." He huffed for a minute. "I can't see how it can be connected though."

"What about his mother? Is she still alive?"

Mom's question was addressed to me, but Greg answered. "I spoke with her earlier." He released a sigh. "I hate doing family notifications over the phone. Anyway, she said she hadn't known that her husband was here. He told her he would be away on business, that's all. Apparently, he wasn't very forthcoming about what he was doing. She's going to be here tomorrow."

"What was he doing here?" I asked again.

Greg fell silent for a minute. "It appears he was trying to buy a winery or two. The realtor was working for him," he finally said. "We found paperwork indicating he bought Two Sisters Winery, and he had made an offer on several vacant properties."

This surprised me. "What would he want with the wineries? He didn't approve of Chase's choice of a career."

Greg shrugged. "I have more questions than answers right now. The desk clerk said he used a credit card and ID with a different name. His wallet was in the room with his correct license in it along with a large amount of cash. It wasn't a robbery gone wrong. So far, we haven't located the phony ID and credit card. They weren't in the room."

"What evidence did you find at the scene that points to

Templeton?" Joe brought our thoughts back on track.

"The weapon used was a knife like I've seen you use around here. The Templeton logo is etched into the blade. Apparently he has that logo etched into every piece of equipment he owns." Rather convenient for the real killer, I thought. It pointed right to Chase. This time I knew enough to keep my mouth shut.

"Any fingerprints?"

Greg didn't answer immediately, thinking over what to say. "The only prints belonged to Chase," he finally said.

"His knife, his prints," Joe stated in his matter-of-fact way. He shrugged, and fell silent again. He only talked when he had something important to say.

"He was stabbed?" Bonnie's voice trembled slightly.

Ty had remained silent throughout this conversation. He looked at Greg waiting to see what he would say. Finally Greg shook his head. "His throat was slashed, nearly decapitating him." That's what Ty had meant by gruesome.

Bonnie and I gasped. Her face had a slightly green tint at this point. I thought she was going to faint. Her sheltered life hadn't prepared her for something like this. I wondered if her parents were keeping track of what was happening in her life. They'd try to make her go home if they were.

"If he was going to kill someone, why use his own knife and leave it at the scene? That implicates him." Mom drew the attention away from the gruesome aspect, hoping to give Bonnie time to recover.

"Okay, okay, I get it. Maybe Pattiann was partway right. I don't like the guy. I wouldn't mind seeing him in a little bit of hot water, but I wouldn't do anything to make him look guilty if he isn't."

"Why don't you like him? He's usually nice." Bonnie spoke softly, giving that qualifier. He hadn't been so nice when he told her she couldn't work for him any longer.

"You don't know him the way we do," Greg said. "He's smug, and he thinks he knows everything. He didn't like it when Skylar bought this place. He tried to discredit her wines until he discovered who her father is. Then he wanted to date her. He didn't like us being together either."

"He's proud of what he's accomplished, and he has every right to be. I think part of his attitude is to cover the fact that he's really lonely. That doesn't make him a murderer." Her logic was so simple, but right on. How had my friend gotten so insightful?

~~~

He was running out of time. He had to finish what he'd started out to do, or this would all have been a big waste. He paced across the room. Well, not everything, he chuckled. One good thing came out of this mess. The old man isn't going to bother anyone again.

He'd been getting soft. He was looking to mend some fences. Of course, he didn't know how to go about doing that. Did he really think he could buy him off? Too much water had gone over that dam. I could have told him that if he'd only asked.

Instead, he came here with the intent of bringing everything under one roof, so to speak. That never would have happened, he thought. But either way it would have ruined my plans.

So where did he go from here? His plan to discredit the competition for the empire hadn't turned out so well. As he continued to pace around the room, a new plan began to form in his mind. It wouldn't be easy, but it just might work. He was going to need a little unwitting help though. He gave a chuckle. This could be fun.
~~~

CHAPTER FOURTEEN

What the hell is she doing here? He watched the woman get out of a big Town Car. He hadn't anticipated her showing up. The fact that her husband had been murdered by his own son, her son, didn't mean anything. They had lived separate lives for years. What did she care? She was free of a tyrant now, as was anyone else who knew the man.

She was going to complicate things that much was certain. But he wouldn't let that stop him. He was going to finish what he started. He'd waited too long for the empire to be his. He wasn't going to let her or anyone else ruin it for him. He turned away. It was time to get on with his plan.

~~~

In the space of a few weeks there had been two murders in town. Major crimes like that didn't happen in New Haven or our small county. The latest murder had the entire town buzzing, and the mayor was fuming over it. For several years he had secretly planned on turning the area in and around New Haven into the next Napa Valley with the resorts that went with it. Murders certainly didn't help the image he was trying to project.

The murders were completely different in the manner of death. I didn't know if that meant they had been committed by different people. If that wasn't the case, why were they both killed? The connecting factor seemed to be Chase. He still claimed he hadn't known Shirley, and hadn't known his father was in New Haven. It wasn't my job to figure that out, I reminded myself as I left work that evening.

Chase's mother had arrived first thing that morning. Greg brought her to the morgue to identify her husband's body. She was a pretty woman in her late fifties, fashionably dressed in a pale pink business suit. She didn't look overly upset by her husband's death. But who was I to judge? People grieve in different ways.
~~~

When the news media had gotten wind of who the latest victim was, they descended on us like a plague of locust. Apparently Charles Templeton was a big deal in the Pacific Northwest, and elsewhere. The fact that he was the father of one of our vintners also drew the media attention. Chase's relationship with the Oregon Templetons had escaped the attention of the media until now.

News vans had set up camp in the hospital parking lot in the hopes of getting someone to give them a statement for the evening news. Mrs. Templeton ignored the microphones and shouts as she breezed in and out of the hospital. It hadn't taken her long to identify her husband's body. I wondered if Chase knew she was in town, or if she would go see her son.

A big Town Car was parked in front of Chase's house when Bonnie and I drove past that evening. "I'll bet that's his mother," Bonnie said. "I wonder what she has to say to him after all these years. My parents aren't exactly the warm and fuzzy type, but at least they didn't disown me because I moved here."

I was gradually learning bits and pieces of her life before coming to New Haven. Her parents had been well into their fifties when she was born. As their only child, they had been overly protective. By the time she was a teenager, they were closer to most grandparent's ages. That could explain why she didn't date any of their friends kids, but why didn't they let her have friends? It must have been difficult for them to deal with a teenager. Their way of doing that had been to isolate her from her peers.

"Do you think Greg found out why those people said Chase was at the hotel that night?" She looked at me hopefully.

I lifted my shoulders in a shrug. "He hasn't been arrested, so maybe Greg realized they were wrong." It was the only explanation I had. I was more curious about Chase's mother. He had said she never opposed her husband. Would she believe her son had killed his father? I hoped not. Maybe with her husband gone, she would feel free to visit Chase now. It would be quite a reunion. I wasn't sure he would want to see her though. I couldn't blame him if he didn't.

Mom had dinner waiting for us when we got there. I was feeling guilty about adding to her work, but she enjoyed having us around. "Your mom is the best," Bonnie whispered as she picked up her fork. "I was never allowed to have friends over. But I didn't have any friends," she added softly.

Her parents hadn't come to visit her since she moved here. They were in their seventies now. That isn't old by today's standards, but if they are in poor health they wouldn't be able to travel. I doubted that they would approve of her friendship with me though.

"What's Greg had to say about Mrs. Templeton?" Mom and Joe had waited to eat until we arrived, and they joined us now. When they were first married I'd worried that Joe wouldn't want to have me around all the time since he'd never had kids. But he enjoyed all the talk, even if he didn't add a lot to the conversation.

"You know your brother," Mom laughed. "I've tried to pry some information out of him, but he isn't very forthcoming."

"That's because it's an open investigation." Greg and Skylar came through the connecting door from the tasting room. Their house was like a duplex, Greg and Skylar on one end, Mom and Joe on the other, with the tasting room in between the two homes.

"Yes, dear, we're aware of that, but it wouldn't hurt to give us a little information. It isn't like we're going to run to the news media with what you tell us." We had never been this closely connected to one of his cases. She was as curious as I was about Chase's mother.

"Did you find out why those people said Chase was at the hotel?" Bonnie cut to the heart of the matter. "He couldn't be in two places at once."

"I know that's what you said, but…" He hesitated. "The desk clerk is familiar with Chase. He's been to the tasting room several times, and felt he knew him well enough to say positively it was him. He even spoke to him as he walked through the lobby. He swears it was Templeton."

I shook my head, but didn't argue further. "What about the hotel guests? How could they identify him?" Tourists wouldn't know him personally.

"They've been here on wine tasting tours a number of times, and had visited his tasting room recently. They felt comfortable saying it was Chase, especially after he acknowledged the desk clerk's greeting. The fact that he was wearing a Templeton Vineyard polo shirt and he looked like Chase, they assumed it was him." Greg sighed.

"You know what assuming does," I said. I'd never seen Chase wear one of his own polo shirts, but that didn't mean he never wore one.

"It couldn't have been Chase," Bonnie insisted. "We saw him at his place when we left here."

Greg gave another sigh. "I know that's what you said, but someone is mistaken. The two of you are his only alibi. If you hadn't seen him that night, he couldn't prove where he was at the time of the murder. I'm just not sure which way a jury would lean."

"So you're saying a jury would take the word of the desk clerk who barely knew Chase and some tourists over ours." I knew this was a possibility. There was no predicting what a jury would do. "They might know what they saw, but so do we."

"He spoke to Chase as he went through the lobby," Greg emphasized.

"Did he actually talk to the man, or just call out to him?" I wasn't sure where I was going with this, but I didn't believe Chase was capable of killing anyone, let alone his father. I didn't like the way he'd treated Bonnie, but that didn't make him a killer.

"I haven't arrested Chase, but I haven't cleared him either. Someone that looked a lot like Chase was at the hotel last night."

Someone that looked like Chase, I thought. This was becoming a common theme. The man I saw outside the theater had looked like Chase. Bonnie had seen him leaving the hospital. Martha said she had seen him in town as well. He'd acted like he didn't know her. He would acknowledge a greeting, but he never stopped to talk to anyone. Did Chase have a double in New Haven? "Could it have been Mr. Templeton that they saw, not Chase?" I suggested. "Maybe he'd gone out to eat, and was returning when they saw him."

"The man registered under a false name," Greg reminded me. "There was no reason for the clerk to call him Chase. He wouldn't have responded with a wave either since he was trying to hide his identity." His sigh was filled with frustration.

"People are susceptible to suggestions," Greg admitted, "even something as simple as the logo on a shirt. That's why we can't rely solely on eye witnesses." So it could have been a tall man with blonde hair wearing a Templeton Vineyard shirt, I thought.

"What about Mrs. Templeton?" Mom asked. "Does she think Chase killed his father?"

He shook his head. "She hasn't seen her son in close to ten years. She has no idea what he's capable of, but she doesn't want to think he'd do something like that."

"What about a motive?" Joe asked. "I might not like the guy, but I can't see him doing something like that without a reason." That was a long speech for him.

Greg shrugged. "If Chase had known what his father was up to, I might say that was motive enough. He maintains he didn't know his father was in town, and had no idea his father was the one trying to buy the wineries. I can't prove otherwise. He said he wouldn't have had anything to do with him if he had known."

"What was Templeton planning on doing with the wineries?"

"Apparently he was trying to take over the wine industry in our little corner of the world. I've talked to the realtor. Templeton Senior never let him in on what he was planning on doing with any wineries once he bought them. He hadn't been aware of his true identity either."

"I don't think Chase would be happy to have his father in competition with him."

Greg shook his head. "That wasn't his plan. He had papers drawn up to incorporate Templeton Vineyards into his own business empire along with any others he bought. Without anything to confirm my suspicions, I'm only guessing that the man thought he could entice Chase back into the fold if he had control of the wine industry here."

I snorted at that. "Chase would never agree to that. Did you tell him about his father's plans?"

"Yeah, I told him." He chuckled. "He went ballistic. If his father wasn't already dead, he would have killed him right then. That would definitely have been a motive to do away with his father before he could execute his plans."

"But Chase couldn't have done it," Bonnie objected again. "We saw him at his place." In spite of the way he had treated her, she was sticking up for him. I wasn't sure I could have done the same in her shoes.

Greg nodded. "I know. I'm just saying he had motive and means. The knife came from his winery. But if you girls are right, and I don't doubt you," he added quickly, "he didn't have the opportunity. I'm still trying to figure out who the guy is that the others saw." He gave a frustrated sigh. "I can't prove Chase knew his father was in town, but I can't disprove it either. I hate it when things don't add up."

"How could he force Chase to agree to go along with his plans?" Skylar asked. "That winery is his pride and joy. He would never turn it over just like that."

Greg shrugged. "That's something we'll never know, I guess. It's easy to see where Chase got his self-important attitude from. Templeton Senior apparently figured he could do anything he wanted without anyone complaining."

"What about the lawyer?" I asked. "Was he working with Mr. Templeton as well?"

Greg shook his head. "I haven't been able to get ahold of him. Apparently he's no longer in town. I think he took off at the first sign of trouble. I've called his office several times, but he isn't returning my calls." He ran his fingers through his hair in a gesture of frustration. "The realtor said he had no dealings with the lawyer, and didn't know anything about him.

"According to hotel employees, Templeton rarely left his room," Greg continued. "The realtor said he'd visited him several times in his hotel room, but no one recalls seeing Chase in the hotel until the day of the murder." When Bonnie and I started to object again, he held up his hand. "Someone was trying hard to make it look like Chase killed his father. Now I just have to figure out who that is, and why they would do that."

Something Chase said at the diner floated around the edges of my memory, but the recent happenings had driven it from my mind. Maybe it would come to me when I least expected it to.

It was getting late when Bonnie and I headed back to town. Passing Templeton Vineyard, I slowed down. The big car was still sitting in front of Chase's house. "It doesn't look like Chase ran her off," Bonnie said. "I hope they can reconnect."

"Maybe with her husband gone, she feels free to see him?" I suggested with a question in my voice. It was the best answer I could come up with.

"You don't think she hired someone to kill her husband, do you?" Her eyes were big in her face. "Maybe she got tired of him telling her what to do all the time." She'd been reading some of my mystery novels, and saw bad guys everywhere now. We fell silent, each of us considering the possibilities.

"I wish I was still working for him. I thought we were going to be friends," she added with a sigh. "I just didn't want to be romantic friends. I guess I didn't handle things very well."

"You didn't do anything wrong," I assured her. "Maybe he didn't know how to handle his own feelings, and went about it all wrong." I hoped that was the case, and he'd realize his mistake and apologize. What difference did it make if she worked for him while they were dating? I doubted that Bonnie would go out with him again even if he apologized.

A new thought struck me then. Maybe he'd found out she was also dating Walt. If that was the case, he might have been hurt. He had built walls around his heart a long time ago. This could be his way of avoiding getting hurt further.

The light traffic on the country roads made it easy to see if someone was following us. I still didn't know what kind of vehicle Rob drove. I wasn't sure what I was going to do if he was the one following me. Greg had enough to worry about right now without me running to him with my problem. I'd replaced the baseball bat that had been stolen out of my car, but wasn't sure what good it would do.

As we got closer to town, I couldn't tell if the same vehicle stayed behind us. It wasn't until I pulled into my driveway that I saw the big truck pull to the curb down the street. My heart jumped into my throat. I wanted to grab the baseball bat out of the backseat and confront the guy, but I knew better. If this was the person following me, it couldn't be Chase. His mother had still been at his place when we drove past just a short time ago. He wouldn't leave her there so he could follow me.

When a man got out of the truck heading up the walk to the house, my heart rate began to slow. There wasn't enough light to see his face, but I could tell he had a beard. A ball cap was pulled low on his forehead. It was probably someone visiting a neighbor. But this late at night?

"What's wrong, Pattiann?" Bonnie stopped beside me, looked down the block. "Do you think that's the guy who's been following you?" Her soft voice trembled slightly.

"It must not be since he's visiting a neighbor. Let's just go inside." I hustled her to the door. She knew I thought someone had been following me. I didn't want to put her in danger if I really did have a stalker. I said a prayer that I hadn't put her in danger by letting her move in with me.

~~~

The best place in any town to pick up gossip is the local watering hole. The beer and pretzel crowd didn't go in for wine, so he wasn't worried about being recognized. The people that frequented such a place probably hadn't been to any of the tasting rooms.

He wasn't taking any chances though. A fake beard, a pair of glasses, and a ball cap were enough of a disguise for now. It wouldn't do to be recognized. He still had some work to do. The one person that knew him best wouldn't be caught dead in a dive like this, so he didn't have to worry about running into her either.

The latest murder was all everyone was talking about. According to the town gossips, those two women had offered an alibi for the time in question. He hadn't expected that. Would that help or hinder his plans? He needed to figure that out before it all went to hell.
~~~

CHAPTER FIFTEEN

Since Bonnie was no longer working for Chase on her days off, she would be helping out at Sky Vineyard. Chase's decision didn't make sense, but a lot of things hadn't been making sense lately.

Before I headed to the winery on Thursday morning, Bonnie and I decided to do a little shopping. She was looking for items she could use to decorate her room. Since she'd rented a furnished apartment, she didn't even have her own bed. The daybed was fine for a few nights, but not long term, so we would be looking for a bed as well.

There were several second-hand stores in New Haven, and we started there. "You sure you don't mind if I change things? It's your house."

"It's your home, too. As long as you don't paint the room black and decorate in skull and cross bones, I don't care what you do."

"Skull and cross bones," she giggled. "Who would do something like that?" I wasn't sure, but there were probably people out there who like that sort of thing. This was another new experience for her. Apparently her parents had even controlled how she decorated her room. I couldn't imagine parents being so domineering.

Instead of going with me that afternoon, she decided to stay home to paint her room. She'd never painted anything before, and I wondered if she'd have more paint on her and the floor than on the walls when I got home.

Lost in my thoughts, I headed out of town. When the traffic thinned, I noticed an old car behind me. I'd seen a similar car on several occasions. Was this the same one? The glare on the windshield kept me from seeing the driver. Slowing down, I hoped the driver would pass me. Instead the car slowed down as well.

Pulling to the side of the road, I waited to see what would

happen next. I laid my trusty baseball bat across my lap in case he decided to get nasty. I was tired of whatever game he was playing. It took only a minute for the car to pull up behind me. I gave a small gasp to see who was behind the wheel.

"Are you all r-r-right? D-d-did something happen to your car?" George hurried up to the driver's side window.

"Why are you following me?" My voice was sharp causing him to recoil. "You scared me."

His face grew red. I couldn't tell if it was because of anger or embarrassment. "I-I-I'm s-s-sorry, P-P-Pattiann," George stammered.

"Slow down, and tell me why you've been following me." I remained in my car with the window rolled only part way down. If he was my stalker, I wasn't going to give him the opportunity to grab me.

"I've been watching out for you." His sing-song voice conquered the stutter. "That man is still following you."

"What man, George?" He'd told me this before, but he never told me who it was. My stomach was in knots by now. Was he using this as an excuse to follow me, or was someone really stalking me? Until this all started, I'd thought of him as a gentle giant. Now I wasn't sure what to think.

His brow crinkled as he tried to come up with an answer. "The man in the big truck," he finally said. "He's been watching you." He paused, looking down as he scuffed the toe of his shoe in the dirt.

"George, look at me." I waited until he looked up. "You need to stop following me."

"But what if he hurts you like someone did Sh-Sh-Shirley." Even using the sing-song voice, he had trouble saying her name.

My heart thundered in my ears at his statement. "Do you know who hurt her?" He shook his head so hard I thought he was going to fall over. "How do you know what happened to her?" Greg hadn't released the cause of death for either Shirley or Mr. Templeton to the press.

He scuffed his feet in the dirt at the side of the road some more before answering. “People don’t see me when I’m around. I hear them say things. A man choked Shirley, and put her in that man’s vineyard. Someone cut that other man’s throat. I don’t want that to happen to you.”

When a big truck pulled to the side of the road behind George’s car, his hands began to shake. “D-d-don’t get out of…” His hands gripped the window so hard I thought it was going to break.

I touched his fingers curled over the edge of the glass. “It’s all right, George. Relax. He’s my friend.” Ty stepped onto the road, allowing my heart rate to settle into a normal rhythm.

“You having car trouble again, Pattiann?” Ty’s voice was tight, but he wasn’t in full protective mode yet. His gaze moved over George before returning to me.

“No, it’s fine. This is George. He works at the hospital. You’ve probably seen him around. George, Ty is a paramedic. He’s my friend. Is this the man you saw following me?”

George shook his head. His face was red with embarrassment now. “I-I-I’m sorry.” Without another word, he hurried back to his old car.

“George, wait.” Opening my door, I called to him, but he wasn’t listening. He was in a hurry to get away.

“You mind telling me what that was all about?” Ty pulled me against him, unmindful of any traffic that passed us.

“I’m not really sure.” I rested my head on his chest. His heart was pounding hard against my ear. “He said he’s seen someone watching me, and he was following me to make sure I was safe.”

“Did he say who was watching you?” I shook my head. “Do you believe him?”

I thought about that for several minutes, before nodding my head. “Yeah, I do,” I said with a sigh. “I’ve seen the same truck behind me several times. I can’t see who’s driving though. George was trying to protect me. He wouldn’t hurt anyone unless they were trying to hurt someone he liked.” I hoped that was the truth. "I don't know who or why anyone would follow me."

"I can think of any number of reasons, and none of them are good. Two people have been murdered. You can't assume this is innocent and nothing to worry about. It sounds like someone is obsessed with you."

"You're overreacting. No one's trying to hurt me." My voice wobbled, putting the lie to my words.

"Someone left a rose on your windshield, keyed your car, and broke the window. Now you're being followed. That sounds a lot like you're being stalked. What does Greg have to say? I can't imagine he's too happy about any of this. I'm surprised he doesn't have a deputy following you." Remembering the third degree he'd received the first time he was with me, he chuckled softly. "I wouldn't want to be that guy when Greg catches him."

When I didn't say anything, he pulled away from me, looking down into my face. "You haven't told him." It was a statement, not a question.

I gave a heavy sigh. "No. That isn't a conversation I want to have. He'd try to make me move in with Mom and Joe. That isn't going to happen."

"At least he should talk to George to find out what he knows," Ty insisted.

"I can see how that would go," I scoffed. "Instead of calmly talking to George, he'd start interrogating him. He'd terrify the poor man. George isn't the bad guy here. He's been trying to protect me. The more stressed he gets, the worse his stutter becomes. Greg would never make sense out of what he says." Was Rob doing these things? I wondered. He was angry enough.

"You still need to tell him." He placed a soft kiss on my lips before releasing me. "I'll follow you. I was going to the vineyard anyway."

"Why? The tasting room isn't open today."

"To see you," he chuckled. Dipping his head, he placed

another kiss on my lips before opening the car door for me to get in.

"So you're going to be following me now," I teased, looking up at him through my lashes. "Should I tell Greg about that, too?"

He chuckled, leaning down to give me another kiss. "You bet," he whispered. "He doesn't terrify me." Standing back, he closed my door. A warm glow filled my heart all the way to the winery. I tried to forget that Ty was going to make me tell Greg what George had said.

It was after noon when we pulled into the long lane leading to the winery. Greg had been gone for hours. If I played my cards right, I'd be gone before he came home for dinner. Telling him that someone was following me wouldn't be pretty. He'd be angry that I hadn't told him sooner. I didn't know who was following me, so there was nothing he could do.

I was tired of him fighting my battles. It was time for me to step up to the plate. I chuckled at my baseball analogy, giving my baseball bat a pat. If I came face to face with the person following me, they were going to feel the full weight of my bat. I still knew how to swing it.

Joe didn't mind Ty's help in the vineyard while I worked with Sky. Racking barrels was a never ending job as wine was moved around. The weather was warm even by southeastern Arizona standards. By midafternoon, we were all ready for a break.

Occasionally I saw Ty watching the thin stream of traffic passing by on the road. Was he watching to see if George was out there, or the person he said was following me? He wasn't convinced that George was harmless.

Luck wasn't on my side, and Greg came home before we were finished for the day. He had accepted the fact that Ty wasn't going anywhere, and no longer tried to intimidate him into leaving me alone. "Well, I think we'd better take off." I said, gathering my purse. I wanted to get out of there.

"Your mom's gonna be disappointed if you two don't stick around," Joe said.

"Yeah, what's your hurry?" Greg frowned at me suspiciously.

"I thought I'd make dinner at home tonight. Bonnie might need some help painting her room, too." Ty frowned at me. Before he could say anything, I rushed on. "I've been here almost every evening since this all began. I thought I'd give you all a break." My chuckle sounded more like a moan.

"Yeah, right, what's up?" Greg's eyebrows lowered over his clear blue eyes. When I didn't say anything, he turned to Ty. "What's going on? You two have plans for tonight? Something you want to tell me about?"

Ty gave me a nudge, tipping his head toward my brother. I frowned at him, but he didn't seem moved by it. "You tell him, or I will."

I flopped down in the swing on the front porch. Drawing a deep breath, I let it out slowly. "All right, already. Traitor," I muttered. "A friend of mine thinks he has seen someone following me." Greg and Joe both shifted around to look out at the road. "He isn't there now. He isn't that obvious."

"Who's this friend?" Greg sat down on the porch railing, his leg swinging back and forth like a pendulum. It was his 'tell' when he was upset about something.

"Just someone that works at the hospital," I said. I didn't want to give him a name. It was a lame effort to protect George from Greg's interrogation.

"Who?" His tone was stern now.

"George Butler," I sighed. "He works in maintenance at the hospital."

"How does he know someone is following you? When did this start?"

There was no way to get out of this. "The night I had dinner with Chase at the diner George thought someone followed me out of the parking lot."

"Chase again," Greg grumbled. "His name's been coming

up a lot lately. He seems to be involved with everything that's going on around here."

"He isn't the one that followed me." At least not that night, I added silently. "If you're going to get all official on me, we can just skip this little talk."

"Not gonna happen. Tell me about this George character. Who does he think is following you?"

Scowling at him, I huffed and puffed before continuing. "He doesn't know who it is. It's someone in a big truck. That's all he can tell me."

"A big truck like Chase drives," he stated.

"That's not what I said." I didn't want to admit the thought had crossed my mind more than once. The truck I'd seen several times was the same color as the one Chase drives. Until I knew what kind of vehicle Rob drove, I couldn't say he wasn't behind this.

"Maybe not, but it's quite a coincidence that he drives the same kind of truck as the one following you. How did this George know someone followed you from the diner if he works at the hospital?"

"He has a second job bussing tables at the diner." It took a long time for me to finish telling about the times I thought someone was following me because of all the interruptions. By that time Mom was home. She got in on the tail end my story. Her face was white with worry.

"Why didn't you tell us before now? The person following you could be a killer."

The butterflies in my stomach began to flutter. "Why would a killer target me?"

"A killer doesn't have to have a reason for what he does," Greg said. "Besides, we don't know why Shirley or Templeton were killed." His jaw was clenched so tight, the muscle in his cheek was like a knot along his jaw. "This could be the guy that keyed your car and broke the window." He turned to Ty. "You knew about this?"

"Now, wait a minute. This isn't Ty's fault," I tried to

intervene before Greg went off the track.

"Not until today." They both ignored me. "If I'd known someone was following her, I would have taken care of it myself." Ty's tone was as sharp as Greg's.

"Stop it, both of you. I don't need anyone fighting my battles for me. I wish you'd just forget it." He didn't need to know about my suspicions of Rob. I could tell Mom wanted to wrap me in cotton batting and lock me away from any harm. I had allowed them to treat me like a child long enough. It was time to take charge of my own life.

"Honey, why didn't you tell us about this before now?" she asked, as she sat down beside me. The hand that gripped mine was icy with fear. "Greg could have stopped whoever is doing this."

"That's just it, Mom. I'm an adult. I figured it was time to put on my big girl panties and take care of my own problems. I shouldn't have to run to my big brother every time something happens."

Greg chuckled, "Big girl panties, huh?"

"You know what I mean." I kicked at his foot still swinging beside me. "You don't have enough deputies to have one of them following me around twenty-four/seven. I've also been around law enforcement long enough to know there's nothing you can do until a crime has been committed. Following someone isn't a crime. Besides, nothing was taken, and there was no sign of forced entry. Oops." I covered my mouth with my hand. I couldn't believe I said that out loud. I'd gotten carried away with my story, and went too far. Ty sat up straight, looking down at me. His eyes were filled with worry, along with a touch of anger.

"Yeah, oops," Greg growled, his face was dark with suppressed anger. "What forced entry? This sounds like a lot more than someone following you. When did this happen?"

"Like I said, nothing was taken. It's no big deal." I couldn't look anyone in the face by this time.

"Someone in your house is a big deal, young lady," Joe

stated, a dark frown drawing his bushy brows together. I remembered that tone from my dad when I'd done something wrong as a little girl. I was feeling very much like that little girl again. I didn't like the feeling.

Ty turned me so I was looking at him. "Someone was in your house, and you never said anything? Why? What if this has something to do with the two murders?" He gave a shudder at the thought.

"I knew you'd been acting squirrely lately." Greg sat down beside Skylar. "When did this happen? I want to know everything. Don't even think about leaving anything out."

A strained silence lasted for several moments while I debated what to say. Whatever I said, it wasn't going to turn out good. "The night after I had dinner with Chase I left here early. I wanted to get home before dark. I was hot and sweaty after working with Skylar all day. When I came back out to the kitchen after my shower, there was a noise on the patio. I thought it was a wild animal, or something."

"It was something all right," Greg mutter. "What would you have done if he'd still been in your house when you walked in?"

"There was nothing to indicate that anyone had been in the house when I got home. Nothing in the living room or kitchen was missing or moved. The door was still locked when I got home, so why would I suspect anyone had been in there?" I left out the part that the back door had been unlocked when I finally got around to checking it.

"But you knew someone had followed you the night before. You should have told me."

"What would you have done? In cases where nothing is stolen, and there is no sign of forced entry, an officer isn't even sent out to take a report. There's nothing you could you."

"This is different. You're my sister."

"I shouldn't get special attention because of that." He started to argue, but I stopped him. "Do you want me to tell this, or are you going to keep interrupting?" Folding his arms over his chest, he clamped his lips tight. "When I finished eating I went into the spare bedroom. Things were scattered all over. I didn't leave it like that either," I quickly added before he could accuse me of leaving the mess myself.

"So why didn't you call me right then?"

"My TV and laptop were there. My jewelry wasn't missing. Even the cash I keep in a drawer was still there." I stressed. "Whoever was in there went through the filing cabinet. There was nothing for them to steal. All of my important papers are locked up at the bank. No windows were broken, and the doors hadn't been forced. What could you have done at that point?" I waited for Greg to say something.

He paced around for a minute before sitting down beside Skylar again. "Have you seen anything to indicate they've been in there since?"

I shook my head. "I make doubly sure the doors and windows are locked before I leave. I don't know how someone could get past the dead bolt locks you installed."

"Where there's a will, there's a way," he said. "I'm going to need to talk to this George. Can he describe the person following you?"

"He wasn't very clear on that point. He said it's sort of the same guy I had dinner with."

"Sort of the same guy, meaning Chase?"

I shrugged. "I don't think he knows. I've never been able to see who it is either."

"You've seen someone following you, and you still didn't say anything." He ran his fingers through his hair. "I thought I'd taught you better than this. Where can I find George?"

"You can't just approach him all official, Greg. You'll scare him to death."

He gave a frustrated sigh. "I'm not going to scare him. If he knows anything about this person following you, I need him to tell me."

"He has a bad stutter. Because of that he's very shy. You'll never get anything out of him."

"Leave that to me. I'll talk to him tomorrow."

When a car turned into the lane, my heart rate jumped, and the three men stood up ready to confront anyone daring enough to enter their territory. Mom held up her hand. "Take it easy, boys. It's just Bonnie." At some point during all this, she had texted Bonnie to come out for dinner.

"Did you even think to warn her about all this?" Greg lifted one eyebrow. "She should know there might be some danger."

"She knows." I had told her up front so she could decide if she still wanted to move in with me.

He wasn't finished with me, but stopped long enough to eat the pizza and wings Bonnie had brought with her.

"Tell me about the truck you've seen following you." He picked up the interrogation as soon as the last slice of pizza was gone. "Is it possible it's Chase?"

"The windows are tinted, so I can't see the driver, but it's a big truck similar to the one Chase drives. I've never seen a logo on it though. His truck has logos on the doors and the tailgate."

"Tell him about the flowers," Ty said. I was ready to kick him next. Was nothing sacred?

"What's this about flowers?" Greg's eyebrows dropped low over his eyes in a glare. "What did the card say?" he asked after I told him about the flower delivery. "When did you get them?"

"It was a month or so ago. There was no signature on the card."

"Are you sure Chase didn't send them?"

"Yeah, I asked him. He didn't."

"He didn't admit sending them," Greg said. "Do you remember what flower shop sent them?" I shook my head. They could have been sent from anywhere. "Okay, I'll talk to George first thing tomorrow."

"No, you won't. This is why I didn't say anything before. If you go all official on him, and you'll scare him so badly he won't even be able to talk."

"I'm not going to scare him. I need to find out what he knows about this guy following you. If it's Chase," his voice was a low growl now, "he's the one that's going to be scared. What time does George start his shift? Do you know where he lives?"

"Let me talk to him first." He started shaking his head, and I rushed on. "You'll never get anything out of him the way you're going about this. If I'm there when you talk to him, it will help."

"Not if this is his way of getting close to you," he objected.

"He wouldn't do something like that. He's a nice guy. It can't hurt to have me there."

It took a little more coaxing and prodding, but he finally gave in. "Okay, but if you interrupt, I'll make you leave. Understood?" I nodded my head, but that wasn't going to happen. "Where can I find him?"

"I know what time he gets off work. You can talk to him then."

"That's not what I asked, Pattiann." He gave me his most intimidating stare.

He's been using that tactic since we were kids. It hadn't worked then, it didn't work now. I crossed my arms over my chest, returning him stare for stare. "I don't know where he lives. He works another job when he finishes at the hospital. If you want to talk to him, you'll have to catch him when he isn't working. I don't want him to lose his job because he was trying to help me."

He finally relented with a sigh. "Okay, you can go with me, but I'm not waiting until he gets off work. We'll go before he starts his shift at the hospital. When did you get so stubborn?"

"I had a good teacher." He chuckled at that, but didn't argue.

I said a prayer that George would be able to tell him more

than he'd told me.

CHAPTER SIXTEEN

Greg was at my front door before I'd had my first cup of coffee the following morning. "I want to talk to this character before he starts his shift," he said. "Let's go." He was eager to find out what George could tell him. I still wasn't convinced this was going to work. Greg could be very intimidating in his uniform.

George's beater car was parked at the back of the hospital lot when we pulled in. "Hi P-p-p-Pattiann," George stuttered when he entered the room. His eyes were as big as saucers when he saw Greg. We had the small waiting room to ourselves for the time being. "D-d-did I d-d-do s-s-something wrong?" He was wringing his hands.

"Everything is fine, George. This is my brother, Greg. He'd just like to ask you a few questions about the man you've seen following me." His head bobbed up and down, but he didn't relax.

Greg cleared his throat. It was his signal for me to shut up. I wasn't going to let him intimidate George though. "Hi, George." He held out his hand in a friendly gesture. "Have a seat. I promise I won't keep you very long so you can get back to work. I just need to know what you can tell me about the person who is following Pattiann."

"N-n-nothing," he stuttered.

The questioning didn't produce any new information. The only description of the man driving the big truck was it sort of looked like the man I'd had dinner with. That meant it looked sort of like Chase. There was a lot of that going around. Getting even that much information was difficult. George couldn't relax enough to get into a sing-song rhythm, and his stutter never cleared up.

"That was almost a waste of time," Greg sighed when we finally left the hospital.

"I told you he would be too scared to say much."

"If he hasn't done anything wrong, what's he scared of?"

"You," I laughed. "You can be very intimidating when you get all official."

"So how come I don't intimidate you?"

"Because you're my brother. If you had let me ask the questions on my own, I could probably make more sense of what he says."

"You aren't a cop."

"And I don't have to be one to ask questions. You said this isn't a trial. It doesn't matter who asks the questions as long as I get some answers."

"Do you think he knows who is following you?"

I shook my head. "If he's seen the same truck I have, the windows are too dark to tell who's driving. I don't think he ever thought of getting the license number until you mentioned it. Maybe he'll do it now."

"I don't want him following this guy. It would be dangerous for him if he's found out. This guy could be a coldblooded killer. I wish you and Bonnie would reconsider, and stay with Mom and Joe. There's an extra room in our end of the house as well."

I was shaking my head before he could finish speaking. "I told you I'm not going to run and hide every time something happens. I'm a big girl now. I have to be able to take care of myself."

"Yes, I know all about your big girl panties." He chuckled. I could feel my face getting hot, but I wasn't going to back down. I had a Louisville Slugger at each door, and in my car. There was even one beside my bed. If someone wanted to do me harm, I'd make sure they'd suffer as well.

A line from a movie popped into my head, something about bringing a knife to a gun fight. I hoped I wasn't bringing a baseball bat to a gun fight.

Greg took me to the winery, and Bonnie showed up before the tasting room opened. Betsy and her husband were on a cruise for the next week, so Bonnie would be working with me.

Minutes before we opened, my phone vibrated in my pocket. Pulling it out to check caller ID, I looked up at Bonnie. I wasn't sure how this conversation was going to go.

"Hello, Chase. What do you want?" There was ice in my voice. I stepped into the back room so Bonnie wouldn't hear what I had to say.

He ignored my harsh tone. "Do you know where Bonnie is? Is she sick? I thought she'd be here by now. She knows what time the tasting room opens. She didn't call to say she'd be late." His words came out in a rush. After what he'd said to her, he had a lot of nerve expecting her to be there. He sounded worried, but about Bonnie or himself, I didn't know. Maybe Bonnie had misunderstood his meaning. I didn't see how that could be though.

"She's here with me. She took what you said the other night seriously. How could you say that to her? You really hurt her feelings."

"What are you talking about? I haven't talked to her since last weekend."

I pulled the phone away to look at it like I could figure out what he was talking about. "Chase, she went out to dinner with you three nights ago."

"No, she didn't," he insisted.

I was getting really annoyed with him now. "You came to the hospital to ask her out."

"I haven't been in town all week. I need her to get over here. There are several cars out front already."

I wasn't going to let him off the hook. "You told her she shouldn't work for you since the two of you are dating."

"What? I didn't tell her that, and we aren't dating. We only went out that one time, and she asked me out." He drew in a calming breath. "Look, Pattiann, I don't know what you're talking about. I don't have time for these games, and I don't have time to argue. I need her to get over here. I'm going to have a room full of tourists, and I'm all alone."

"You've handled the tasting room by yourself before. What makes this any different?"

"A lot of these people will be asking questions about my father's murder. I wasn't planning on being front and center today. Who knew being a murder suspect would pull in the tourists?" he grumbled. "I need her here today."

Of course, this was all about him, I thought. This was the pompous, self-centered man Greg and Joe always talked about. "Chase, you told her she couldn't work for you because you were dating," I repeated slowly in case he didn't understand what I said.

"I told you I've only been out with her once. What difference would it make if she worked for me, and we were dating?" It sounded like his jaws were clenched tight.

"Bonnie wouldn't lie about this."

"But you think I would. Has this whole town gone crazy? I didn't tell she couldn't work for me, and I'm not dating her. What am I supposed to do without any help today?"

"Well, I don't know." Sarcasm dripped from my voice. "For starters, you might want to call and apologize to her."

"For what? I didn't do anything." His voice was climbing in volume, and I pulled the phone away from my ear.

He sounded sincere, but I know Bonnie went out with him just the other night. "I'll talk to her and see what she has to say. I can't guarantee anything." I disconnected before he could argue further.

"How could he forget we went out to dinner?" Bonnie asked after I explained about the call. A confused frown drew her eyebrows together. "It must not have been a very memorable evening for him. It's one I'll never forget. Should I go over to help him?" She was wringing her hands.

"You don't have to go over there if you don't want to," Sky said. "Chase always looks out for number one. He can't get away with treating people badly."

"Why wouldn't he remember saying those things to me?"

"Some people only remember what's useful to them," Sky

said with a shrug.

Before she could make up her mind, her phone buzzed. Looking at caller ID, her eyes got round as dollars. "It's Chase," she whispered, as though he could hear her. "What do I say to him?"

"Answer the phone and see what he has to say for himself."

"Hello?" Her voice was timid and soft. "Yes. Okay." She paused between each word, listening to what he had to say. He must have been convincing. "All right, I'll check with Sky. If she doesn't need me here, I'll be over. Are you sure you still want me to work for you?" Another pause and she disconnected without saying anything else.

"He said we didn't go out to dinner this week, and he would never say those things to me. If it wasn't Chase, who did I go out with?" Worry wrinkled her forehead. "He said he doesn't have anyone to help him today, and there are people waiting to get in. What if there are still reporters around. What would I say to them?"

"Don't tell them anything," I said. "If they keep pressing you, call the sheriff's office. I'm sure Chase has security there as well."

"Okay," she sighed. "I guess I'll go over to help him if you're sure you don't need me here." She looked at Sky. I thought she was hoping Sky would tell her she was needed here. "He sounded sort of desperate."

"Pattiann and I can handle things here, but you don't have to go over there. Chase can deal with things on his own."

She thought about that for a minute, before giving a sigh. "I guess I should go. He's depending on me." Once again I thought she was too nice for her own good at times. She turned to me. "I'll pick you up after we close."

"If he so much as says one thing out of line, you come right back here. Don't let him push you around." I gave her a hug before she left. I was feeling very protective of her. Maybe this was how Greg felt about me. She headed out to her car looking like she was going to her own doom.

"How could he forget about their date? Or is he pretending so she'll help him out today?" I looked at Sky hoping she could fill in some answers.

"He's been acting really weird lately," Sky said. "What difference would it make if they were dating? She could still work there." She shook her head. She hadn't pulled her long hair into a ponytail yet, and it fell into her face. "I don't know what's up with him. I saw him in town last week, and he walked past people without as much as saying hello. I know he has a lot on his mind with his father being murdered, and his mother being in town, but that's still odd." I had to agree with her, but it was time for a subject change.

"Do you know if she's still here? What did Greg have to say about her?"

"She had very little to say to Greg. She didn't seem upset by her husband's death. I'm assuming she claimed his body, and left. I don't even know if she went to see Chase."

"Yeah, I think she did," I nodded, explaining about the big car parked in front of his house the night she came to town. "Why would she leave so quickly? You would think she'd want to spend time with her son since she hasn't seen him for such a long time." I said. I couldn't imagine being so isolated from my family.

A new thought began to take root in my mind as the day wore on. Too many people had seen Chase in town without any recognition from him. Before I said anything, I needed to check something out on the internet. I couldn't wait to get home to my computer.

"How did things go?" Bonnie looked frazzled when she came to get me at the end of the day. It had been busy, but I was certain Chase could have handled it by himself. He just didn't want to. "Were there any reporters?"

She shrugged. "If there were, they pretended to be customers. Most everybody had heard about the murders, and asked a lot of questions. Everyone was really nosey. I pretended like I didn't know what they were talking about. I think they wanted to see what a real murderer looked like." She gave a sigh. "Sales were good though," she said trying to look on the bright side. "Getting wine made by a possible killer must be popular. I think the whole world has gone topsy-turvy.

"They didn't get a look at him though," she continued. "He stayed in the back room, leaving me to handle everything. He swears we didn't go on a date three nights ago. Who did I go out with if it wasn't him?" She brushed her bangs out of her face. "Am I going crazy? Did I go on a date with someone else, and just thought it was Chase?"

I didn't have an answer for her right then. I was going to do some research when we got home. Maybe then I could figure out what was going on with him.

~~~

All the tension between her and Chase, and working by herself all day, Bonnie was tired. Instead of going home immediately, we decided to relax on the porch with Mom and Joe before heading home. Ty and Walt were on shift, so we wouldn't be hurrying home for a date. When Chase's big truck barreled down the lane, gravel and dust filled the air.

"What the hell are you doing, Templeton?" Joe came off the chair ready for a fight. He'd had enough of Chase to last a lifetime. "You trying to kill someone with that big truck?" We waved our hands in front of our faces to clear the dust in the air. He wasn't convinced that Chase wasn't the one following me either.

His truck looked very much like the one that had parked down the street from my house a few nights ago.

"Where's Greg? I need to talk to him." He ignored Joe. His eyes were wild. "Someone is trying to extort money from me."

"He isn't home from work yet," Skylar said. "Did you call the dispatcher?" Chase was pacing around like a caged animal.

"Didn't you hear me? Someone is trying to extort money
~~~

from me. A dead body is put in my vineyard, my place is broken into, and my father is murdered with a knife from my barn. And now this. What's going to happen next?" He ran his fingers through his hair, causing it to stand straight up.

"Who's trying to extort money from you? Why would they do that?"

"Because he's a crooked lawyer, that's why. I need to talk to Greg. He has to arrest this guy."

"What lawyer?" Skylar frowned. "Is he the same one who was trying to buy up the wineries around here?"

"How would I know?" he snapped. "I never saw that guy. He waited until Bonnie left before he started pounding on my door. I think he was spying on me. He claims I owe him a boat load of money. I told him I didn't owe him anything, but he kept insisting I did. He said he was going to sue me if I didn't pay him what he's got coming. I need to talk to Greg."

"Call his office," Joe said, stepping up behind Skylar. "He isn't here." Bonnie and I moved to stand next to them, and even Cody stood with us presenting a united front. Chase had been acting so erratic lately there was no telling what he would do next.

He continued pacing as he took his cell phone off his belt, hitting 9-1-1. "This is Chase Templeton," he growled when the dispatcher answered. "I need to speak to the sheriff." This was the man Joe and Skylar always talked about. Self-important, pompous, and rude. He was acting like everyone should drop what they were doing and jump to do his bidding.

Greg took his time coming home to take Chase's complaint. He wanted to send a deputy, but Chase had demanded Greg come himself. "All right, I'm here. Tell me about this lawyer."

"He came to my place demanding money. He said I hired him to buy up the wineries around here."

"Did you?" One eyebrow lifted slightly.

"No! Why would I do something like that? I already have my winery. I don't need another one."

"You wanted this place, and tried to run Skylar off when she first moved here. Why wouldn't you try to buy out the competition now?"

Chase's face turned pink, but he dismissed Greg's taunt with a flick of his hand. "That was different. Can't you see someone is trying to frame me for everything that's going on? I didn't kill that woman or my father. And I certainly didn't hire some sleazy lawyer to buy any of the wineries around here. I have enough work. I don't need to add any more. He was probably working for my father."

"No, your father hired a realtor, not a lawyer. He wouldn't need both. What proof does this guy have that you hired him?"

"How would I know? Isn't it your job to figure that out?" He continued pacing, too agitated to sit down.

"What did you tell him?" Greg was relaxing in the swing beside Skylar, watching Chase as he paced back and forth. I thought he was enjoying himself a little too much.

"I told him I didn't hire him, and I didn't owe him anything. He kept demanding I pay up. Are you just going to just sit there?" Chase glared at Greg. "Why aren't you questioning that lawyer instead of me?"

"Well, I have to get all the pertinent information from you before I go question him. Did he say when you hired him? Supposedly, hired him," he quickly corrected himself when Chase started to complain.

"I didn't exactly sit down and have a conversation with him. When he started demanding I pay him, I told him to get lost. I also told him I was going to report him to the sheriff, and that's what I'm doing. Now you need to do your job." He dropped the lawyer's business card on the small wicker table before stomping down the steps to his truck. Dust and gravel spewed out from under the tires again as he sped down the lane.

"Phew," Greg wiped imaginary sweat off his forehead. "He's got himself worked up into a real frenzy." He chuckled.

I took in every detail of his truck until it was out of sight.

The Templeton Vineyard logo was prominently stenciled on each door, and the tailgate. It had been too dark the other times I'd seen the big truck to tell if it had the same logo. Did Chase have two trucks? It didn't make sense that he would.

Greg picked up the business card Chase had left behind. "Well, at least I know the lawyer's back in town." He read the name of the lawyer who had been to see Skylar several times. "Maybe I can talk to him now. He's probably staying at the hotel in town."

"Do you think Chase hired him, and is trying to weasel out of paying him now?" Skylar asked.

Greg shook his head. "Anything is possible, but I don't think Templeton is stupid enough to try something like that. If this guy is any kind of an attorney," he flicked his finger on the card making it snap, "he had his client, whether it's Chase or someone else, sign a contract."

"If he's trying to collect his fees from Chase, he must think Chase is his client," I said.

"What if Chase isn't the one that hired him? Can you hire an attorney by mail or fax?" Sky's voice was soft, remembering something similar had happened to her a year ago. At that time a man, claiming to be her, hired a realtor to sell her winery, all through e-mail and fax. It had almost worked.

Greg pulled her to his side, placing a kiss on her forehead. "We'll get to the bottom of this. It's not something you need to worry about." Easy for him to say, I thought.

"I guess I'd better go find this lawyer before Chase has a coronary." He chuckled. He was enjoying Chase's dilemma.

"Dissociative Identity Disorder, previously known as Multiple Personality Disorder, is a condition where two or more distinct personalities are present in an individual." There were a number of articles giving the description on the internet. I read all I could find online and in my medical text books. The condition often appears in victims of abuse. His father had been domineering, but I didn't know if he had abused Chase as a child.

Often, the person with this disorder has no memory of doing things while in the other personality state. That would account for Chase not remembering having dinner with Bonnie, or what he told her.

It would also account for the fact that he didn't recognize people he should know in town. But they are generally separate personalities. The man claimed to be Chase when Bonnie had dinner with him. That didn't fit the disorder description. Closing my laptop, I was as confused as when I started my research. It would also explain about the attorney. Maybe the other personality had hired the lawyer.

If Chase was having a psychotic break, I didn't want him to get violent with Bonnie. Is that what happened to Shirley? Had he gone out with her, and something caused him to snap? She had worked in Portland where his family is from. If she knew about his family, and tried to use that connection to get something from him, would that cause him to turn violent? There weren't a lot of answers on the internet.

CHAPTER SEVENTEEN

"Samuel Earnhardt, Attorney at Law, is so full of himself," Greg stated. It hadn't taken him long to interview the man. "He swears that Chase Templeton hired him to buy as many wineries as possible. He even gave him a list to follow. According to him, Chase was attempting to take over the local wine business. Sound familiar?" One eyebrow lifted slightly. "That's what Templeton Senior was trying to do."

Every time someone called Chase's father that something tugged at my memory. My train of thought was always interrupted, so I couldn't follow the thread in my mind long enough to figure out what I was missing.

"Did he meet face-to-face with him?" Skylar asked.

Greg nodded his head. "I'd say Chase had a case if it had all been done by e-mail and fax, but this guy says he met with Chase several times. Most of their dealings were by phone though. After stopping there tonight, he said it's the same guy that hired him." He shrugged. "It's his word against Chase. I don't know how Chase is going to get out of this one."

"Did he go to the winery, or meet somewhere else?" Joe asked the question.

"They always met in Benson," Greg admitted. "He claimed Chase didn't want anyone to know what he was up to until it was a done deal." He sighed. "I know what you're getting at. It sounds like someone is trying to frame Chase. But Earnhardt swears the man he met with last night is the same guy he met with previously. He's sticking with that story."

If he had the disorder I'd researched the night before, Chase might be able to use that as a defense. If that isn't the case, I agreed with Greg. Chase wasn't going to be able to get out of paying. But why would he want to buy up the other wineries?

The reason the wineries were profitable, besides the fact

they made excellent wine, was the large number of tourists the different wineries brought in. If there was only one tasting room, people wouldn't be willing to make the drive from Phoenix, Tucson, or other parts of the state.

"Did Templeton sign a contract?" Joe asked.

"Well now, that's another story. Earnhardt was a little hazy on the details of his arrangement with Chase. He claims he has a contract, but he couldn't produce it. Said it was in his office in Phoenix," he chuckled. "He's going to tough it out in the hopes Chase won't want to be drug through the media frenzy of a court case. My thought is to let them fight it out in court. If Earnhardt has a signed contract he can produce, he doesn't have anything to worry about. Otherwise," he left the sentence unfinished.

Chase wouldn't be happy with that decision. My opinion of him kept changing from one day to the next. I had liked the rather shy, sort of modest guy I'd had dinner with. Could that really be less than a month ago? He had been demanding and erratic in behavior lately. It was like he was two different people. That fit the description of the personality disorder I'd researched.

Saturday was another busy day. Chase still wanted Bonnie to run the tasting room for him. Until this mess was cleared up, he was being a coward and staying out of the public eye. I didn't know how I was going to figure out if he had the personality disorder, but it was looking more and more like I was correct. He continued to deny having dinner with Bonnie last week.

Sunday morning always started with church. Bonnie was going with me on a regular basis now. It was part of her upbringing her parents had ignored. "It's the one calm place in the middle of all this," she whispered to me. I knew what she meant. With two murders and the problem at the hospital, we welcomed the calm that knowing God was with us brought. When Ty and Walt weren't on shift they joined us. Our family group was growing. Before long we would take up an entire row.

A tall, thin woman came in alone late in the day on Sunday. It was sort of odd for a woman to come in alone, but I dismissed the thought. Everyone was acting odd lately. Standing at the back of the room, she waited until everyone else had left before approaching the tasting bar. “Is Pattiann Douglas here?” Her voice was soft.

“That’s me.” I smiled at her. I tried to remember if I’d seen her before, but came up empty.

“My name is Jillian Brown.” She watched me for any reaction.

The name didn’t ring any bells. I held out my hand, hoping she’d enlighten me. “It’s nice to meet you. Are you here for wine tasting?”

“Um, no, yes,” she changed her mind. “What do you recommend?”

I gave her the wine list, explaining which ones were dry, sweet, and semi-sweet. “If you like sweet wine, the peach is very good. It’s made from the peaches Skylar grows here on the property.” It was my standard speech, and I was hoping it would help her relax. I still didn’t know who she was, or why she had asked for me.

“Fine, I’d like a glass of the peach wine. Is there some place that we can talk?” Maybe she came here to talk, not taste the wine. There was a hostile air coming from her.

“What’s this about?” I frowned at her. I wasn’t going anywhere until she explained herself.

“You don’t know who I am?”

“No, should I?” I didn’t recall seeing her in town either. New Haven is small. I might not know everyone personally, but at one time or another I’ve seen most of them.

She paused for a long moment. “No, I suppose not. I’m Rob’s girlfriend. Or I was until recently,” she corrected.

I drew in a sharp breath. This wasn’t going to be good. “Okay, what can I do for you?” I could hear the wariness in my voice. Unsure what she was going to do, I stayed behind the bar. "Do you still want the wine?" Her light brown hair was pulled back in a ponytail low on her neck. She wore no makeup. Her eyes were dark brown, almost black. She appeared to be several years older than Rob. This wasn't what I'd pictured his girlfriend to look like.

"Yes, please. Could we talk for a few minutes?" Since there were no other customers, she pointed at the chairs and loveseat across the room. The hostility was still there, but not quite as strong as when she first spoke to me.

She didn't look dangerous, but I remained on guard. I didn't have my baseball bat with me. She was taller than me, but I figured I could take her if she decided to get violent. Unless she had a gun in that oversized purse she was carrying, I amended. Besides, Joe and Skylar were here. Sensing my nervousness, Cody had come to stand beside me. He wouldn't let anything happen to me either.

"Is everything all right?" Skylar had been restocking the shelves, but came over to the bar now. Stepping up to Jillian, she held out her hand. "I'm Skylar Bishop. Is everything okay?" Enough troubles had plagued her in the past couple of years. She wasn't going to take any chances.

Jillian studied me for several moments before saying anything else. "I wanted to know what you could tell me about that woman at the hospital. The one that was killed," she qualified.

This can't be good, I thought. I didn't know how much she knew about Rob's involvement with Shirley. He already blamed me for the breakup. He certainly wasn't going to like Jill talking to me.

"It's been in the paper that she had been sexually harassing some of the men at the hospital." Her tone was slightly accusatory. "Rob told me he wasn't involved with her, but I don't know what to believe." Greg had been upset when that piece of news reached the papers. Apparently, someone at the hospital had leaked it to the media. Probably one of the men she had been harassing.

"Why do you think I would know anything?" Stepping out from behind the bar, Skylar and I joined her in the seating area across the room. Cody stayed right beside me He wasn't taking any chances either.

"The night I called off our engagement, Rob was very upset." She took a sip of the wine I'd poured for her. A look of surprise lit up her face. Apparently she hadn't expected it to be good.

"You were engaged to him?" Rob had called her his girlfriend. He had blamed me for ruining his plans. Had he meant his wedding plans? I glanced at her hands folded in her lap. There was a ring on her right hand with a diamond the size of a large marble. If this had been her engagement ring, I didn't know how Rob could have afforded it.

"Yes," she nodded her head. "We were keeping it quiet until after he graduated. My father didn't approve of Rob." She had the superior air of so many wealthy people. "He thought Rob was a fortune hunter." She gave a little chuckle. "A woman is called a gold digger when she dates a rich man. Men are called fortune hunters." She shook her head. "Never mind. When he left my house that night, he was cursing someone named Pattiann. I thought maybe that was another woman he was seeing."

I was quick to dissuade her of that idea. "I wasn't dating him then or now."

She ignored my comment. "It took some digging, but I finally learned your name. Your brother is the sheriff." I nodded my head this time. If she knew I wasn't after her man, I didn't understand what she wanted with me. I was still picking up on a hostile vibe coming from her.

"Rob had become very jumpy and secretive in the last month or so. He said he was just worried about his classes. But I thought there was more to it than that. His grades have been good until recently. He thought getting hired as a nurse at the hospital would improve my father's opinion of him." Somehow I doubted it would help. I doubted she had a very high opinion of him either.

"When I heard what that woman had been doing, I asked him if that was why he was so upset. He became very defensive and denied any involvement with her. He was protesting a little too strenuously. I think he was lying. I was hoping you could tell me the truth about what happened between them."

"I'm sorry, Jillian, but you're asking the wrong person. You need to talk to Rob." I wasn't going to get in the middle of their trouble.

She glared at me for a moment. That wasn't the answer she was looking for. "Rob had been involved with another woman when I met him. He told me he broke up with her, but I didn't believe him. My father said he had discovered he was still seeing her for several months after we began dating." She gave another sigh. "My father is very protective of me." There was a lot of that going around. I wondered if it was her or his money he was protecting.

"What would you have done if he had said she had been harassing him?"

She didn't need to think about her answer. "Well, I suppose that depends on whether he gave in to her demands. That would be a deal breaker."

"But you broke up with him anyway," I pointed out.

"Yes, I did. I don't think he was telling me the truth. If he was really in fear of losing his job, why wouldn't he report what she was doing?"

"Because he *was* afraid of losing his job," I stated.

She turned angry eyes back on me. "Why are you defending him?

"Because he isn't at fault here." I had been telling him to report what she did, but I didn't blame him for giving in. That was something I couldn't tell Jill. She already blamed him for Shirley harassing him. What would she do if she knew he gave in to her demands?

"So you say. Was she threatening him?"

"This is a conversation you should be having with Rob, not me."

"Why wouldn't he tell me the truth? Why won't you? What are you hiding?"

This conversation was getting out of hand. "I'm not hiding anything." No matter what, she would have ended their relationship. That didn't seem fair. I was beginning to understand where Rob was coming from. What I didn't understand was why he wanted to marry her in the first place. I thought she would always hold her money as a prod to get him to do whatever she wanted.

"Would you blame a rape victim for what happened to her?" I asked.

"That's different."

"Not really." I wanted to point out her double standard. "You don't hear much about women harassing men in the workplace, but it doesn't make much difference which one does the harassing. It's still wrong. It's about the power someone has over those working for them."

"Do you think he killed her?"

I wasn't prepared for that question. Instead of answering, I turned the question back on her. "Do you think he is capable of killing someone?"

"No, I suppose not." Her answer held little conviction. "But how is one to tell what another person is capable of doing?" She sounded so pompous I wanted to smack her.

"Why did you break up with him?"

"A marriage without trust won't last long. I'm not sure I can trust him. Why would she harass him? What did he do that made her think she could get away with it?

"He didn't have to do anything. This is about power, not sex." I felt I was arguing with a deaf person.

"He should have been honest with me, and I don't believe he was."

"Maybe he was afraid you would react exactly the way you did if he told you the truth," Skylar spoke up for the first time.

"Yes, you're probably right. I've always listened to my father's advice. He said Rob wasn't right for me."

"Do you want to give him a second chance?"

She was silent for several moments. "Probably not. I should have listened to my father in the first place. He didn't want me getting involved with Rob." I wasn't the only one that needed to put on her big girl panties.

She set down her empty glass on the flat-topped trunk Skylar was using as a coffee table, and stood up. "Thank you for the wine. It was very good. Maybe I'll bring my father back some time. I'm sure he would enjoy it as well." She left without bothering to pay for the glass of wine. I didn't know how Rob had gotten tangled up with the likes of her.

Skylar and I stared at her retreating back with our mouths hanging open. The wealthy have a different set of etiquette rules than the rest of us. Still I couldn't believe she wouldn't offer to pay for the glass of wine. We watched as she slipped behind the wheel of a fancy BMW. "Do you know who her father is?" I looked at Skylar.

She shook her head. "Brown is a common name, but I don't know of anyone in New Haven by that name." She gave a little laugh. "I don't think anyone in town drives a Beamer either. They could be from one of the other towns close by, and I wouldn't know them. I'd say her daddy has more money than good sense. I wonder if he's trying to protect her, or his money, from fortune hunters. What do you know about this Rob guy?"

I shrugged. "I thought he was a nice guy until he started…" I cut off the sentence. I hadn't said anything about his threats. It wouldn't be good to do it now.

"Started what?" She lifted one eyebrow.

"Nothing." I couldn't look her in the eye.

"Is this something Greg should know about?"

"No, yes, maybe," I couldn't decide which was the right answer. "Please don't say anything to him. He already has enough to worry about. I'm being careful. Honest." After meeting Jill, I could understand why Rob didn't want anyone to know that Shirley was threatening his job. Jillian had as much as said that it was his fault that Shirley had been harassing him.

She sighed. "I guess. I just hope it doesn't come back and bite both of us." For several minutes we were lost in our own thoughts. Finally, she picked up the glass, heading to the sink behind the tasting bar. "Do you think you convinced her that you had nothing to do with Rob?" She looked over her shoulder at me.

"Oh, you picked up on that, too. She'll have to go home and ask her father what he thinks. I doubt she's had a single independent thought in her entire life. As long as she lets daddy make her decisions, she's never going to get married either. They're both afraid some fortune hunter is going to come along and take it all away." I shook my head. Money doesn't buy happiness, and lots of money usually produces paranoia.

If Rob had been counting on marrying into money that explained why he was so upset about the breakup. In my estimation, he'd dodged a pretty nasty bullet. I couldn't imagine they would have had a happy life together as long as her father held the purse strings.

~~~

After the weekend we'd had, Bonnie and I were glad to get back to work. I could deal with patients and a bossy head nurse better than I could with all the drama that was going on at the wineries.

Ty had been on duty all weekend, and I hadn't seen him. He was waiting for me when I walked up to the employee entrance. Without saying anything, he placed a soft kiss on my lips. For a long moment he simply held me close to his hard chest. When he released me, he pulled a small plastic bag out of his pocket, handing it to me. There was a slip of paper inside.
~~~

"What's this?" I frowned at him.

"Read it."

Turning the bag over, I read the few words scrawled there. *"Do you know what your girlfriend does while you're working?"*

"Where did this come from?"

"Someone left it under the windshield wiper on my truck. Do you know who would have left it there?"

I took a step back, looking into his handsome face. "Are you accusing me of something?"

"No!" He scrubbed at his face. "I'm sorry. I didn't mean for it to sound like that. I just wanted to know if you might know who would leave something like this."

I could guess, but I kept that thought to myself. The fact that he had put the paper in a plastic bag meant he thought it was evidence of some kind. "Obviously someone isn't happy with the fact that we're dating." I tipped my head to one side. "Maybe you have a jilted girlfriend, and she doesn't like the fact that you're seeing me."

He shook his head. "I haven't been back in town long enough to have many girlfriends. Six years in the Air Force means all my old girlfriends have moved on to greener pastures." He rubbed at his face again, releasing a sigh. "I was thinking this has something to do with the guy who's following you. It looks like he's stepping up his game."

My first thought had been Rob was doing this as some sort of retaliation for Jill breaking up with him. I hadn't thought about the person following me. I didn't know if Rob was behind that either. "Are you going to show it to Greg?" He nodded his head. "Please, don't. He has enough going on with two murders. He doesn't need to be worried about me. I'm sure it's just some prank."

He thought about that for a moment before nodding his head. "I'll hold off until tonight. I'm off for the next few days. How about dinner? I'll pick something up at Manuel's, and we can discuss it then." I quickly agreed. I wasn't going to turn down my favorite food.

"I think Walt is going to call Bonnie. Maybe we'll be alone for a few minutes." He wiggled his eyebrows suggestively. With another heart-stopping kiss, I sent him home to get some rest. I had all day to look forward to what the evening might bring.

CHAPTER EIGHTEEN

Who left that note for Ty? Would Rob be angry enough to do something that childish? I didn't know how this sort of thing could benefit him though. I debated whether I should confront him. He was still upset with me. Asking him about this would only make it worse. I wanted to tell him that he was better off without Jill. But I doubted he'd believe me.

If the person following me had left the note and stepped up his game as Ty suggested, this could become dangerous very fast. I decided to wait until I could talk it over with Ty before making any decision.

The hospital administration was still being closed-mouth about whether drugs were missing on Shirley's watch. A class on sexual harassment had been initiated, and it was mandatory for all employees to attend. That wasn't sitting well with some of the employees, one in particular.

"Those of us being harassed shouldn't be forced to attend something like that. We're the victims, not the ones doing the harassing." He was playing the victim card for all it was worth. He actually was one of several victims in Shirley's crime, but he was the only one protesting.

"The victims need to feel safe reporting this sort of behavior," Martha told him more than once. "That's what part of this class is about."

I was still hoping to learn a little more about Dissociative Identity Disorder before I mentioned the possibility of something like that to Greg. It wouldn't be his call whether to consider such a thing as a defense. That would be up to the lawyers. If Chase had that disorder, he wasn't responsible for what happened. At least the Chase personality wasn't. I was making myself confused.

In a small hospital, there isn't as much call for psychiatrists as there is in a larger hospital. When the need arises, we can contact one of the larger hospitals close by.

I lucked out when Dr. Granger came in to see a patient later that day. "Do you have a patient you want to refer?" He looked down his patrician nose at me like he'd just encountered a bug. Maybe I wasn't so lucky after all. In his late fifties with a head full of snowy white hair, he usually didn't bother talking to a nurse unless it was to issue an order.

"No, I saw something about the disorder on television." I had an excuse for asking all ready. "I did some checking online, but it wasn't very thorough." I hoped he couldn't see through my lie.

"You ought to know that the internet isn't the most reliable place to seek answers to anything, especially not something as complex as a psychological disorder," he replied in a haughty tone. "If you're interested in studying the condition, I have several text books that might help, but they are very technical." I gritted my teeth at his condescending attitude. He was questioning my ability to comprehend something as lofty as his specialty. "I hope you aren't trying to diagnose a patient. It's best to leave that to the professionals."

I gritted my teeth to keep from saying something inappropriate. Some doctors develop a god-like complex. Specialists are the worst. In their opinion, no one comes close to knowing what they know. "No sir, I'm not trying to diagnose anyone. I thought it sounded fascinating, and wondered how it was diagnosed in a patient. What the symptoms are." Maybe playing up to his ego would get me some answers.

"It isn't something I can explain standing in the hallway. If you're really interested, there are several good classes you can take at the university in Tucson." With that, he sailed down the hall. So much for trying to figure out if that could explain Chase's recent erratic behavior.

Several times throughout the day I felt Rob's gaze trained on me. I wondered whether Jill would contact him after she had visited me. I didn't know how he would react if she did. One way or the other, he would still blame me if she didn't take him back.

When Ty pulled into my driveway behind me that evening, he looked better than he had that morning. Walt's big SUV followed close behind. Ty brushed his lips across mine as he pulled me to his side.

"Hey, Pattiann, how are you?" Walt's question was for me, but he was looking at Bonnie as she stepped out of my car. Until the murders were solved, we were still riding together. Safety in numbers, I guess.

"I'm fine. Are you and Bonnie joining us this evening?" That would prolong the discussion about the note. I still hadn't decided whether to tell Ty about the veiled threats Rob had made.

"No. Actually I was hoping I could convince your roommate to have dinner with me tonight. I know it's kind of short notice, but I just came off shift."

A shy smile curved her lips, and she was tongue-tied for a moment. He was the reason she hadn't wanted to date Chase. Walt was a nice guy. I hope he realized how inexperienced she was. Although she hadn't been romantically interested in Chase, her feelings had been hurt when he said she couldn't work for him. I didn't want her to get hurt again. But it wasn't my place to tell him about her background. That could cause a whole different set of problems.

A bright smile lit up her face. "No, I'm not busy, and yes, I'd like to have dinner with you." She looked down at the scrubs she had on. They had Mickey Mouse and Goofy figures all over them. "Can you give me a few minutes to change first?"

"Sure, no hurry." He breathed a sigh of relief. Maybe he was as taken with her as she was with him. I hoped he'd take things slow.

Once we were alone, Ty pulled me in for a long kiss. Lifting his head, he rested his forehead against mine. "I thought they'd never leave." When my stomach growled, he laughed, and stepped back. "I guess we'd better eat before you drop over from hunger." He helped me spread out the food on the kitchen table.

As always, lunch was nothing more than a distant memory. After a prayer of thanks, we dug in. "Thanks for picking this up. It's been a long time since lunch." There was enough food for four people, but I thought we could put a good dent in it.

When we finished cleaning up the few dishes we'd used, I led the way out to the front porch. The night temperatures had cooled off, but with his arm draped over my shoulders I didn't need to worry about getting a chill.

"You ready to tell me what you've been holding back?" He hadn't forgotten about the note.

Unlike Greg, he listened to what I had to say without interrupting. "He didn't want me to say anything, but after Shirley was murdered I didn't have a choice. When his girlfriend broke up with him over this, he blamed me."

"Why would she do that? Yes, he shouldn't have given in to her demands. But if he felt the threat of losing his job was real, I can understand his decision. Sort of," he qualified.

I think I understood what he was saying. If Rob was insecure of his position, he would do anything to keep it. After meeting Jill, she and her father would be enough to make anyone insecure.

"What about those threats?" he asked. "Are they real, or is he just blowing off steam?"

"I don't have an answer for that. Until this all started, I would have said he would never hurt anyone." I shrugged. "Now I don't know."

"Do you think he was capable of killing Shirley to put an end to the harassment?"

Without thinking about my answer, I shook my head. "He was upset enough to damage my car, but I can't believe he would kill someone."

"You know I have to give the note to Greg," he said quietly. "He isn't going to be happy that I held off this long. As soon as I found it, I put it in the baggie to preserve any fingerprints on the paper. Maybe that will earn me some points." He chuckled.

Instead of waiting until the morning, we decided to drive out to the winery. As predicted, Greg was upset with both of us. "Why didn't you tell me all this when it happened?"

"You had enough to handle without adding my petty problems to the mix. I didn't think Rob would hurt me or anyone else. The note isn't his style either."

He huffed and puffed for a few minutes, but finally relaxed. "All right, I'll talk to him. I suppose you want in on that conversation, too."

I shook my head. "That one you can handle on your own. Just don't accuse him of anything."

When his eyes narrowed at me, I figured I'd stepped in it again. "I don't make a habit of accusing people of something without evidence."

"That's not what I meant. He's having a rough time right now, and he figures I'm to blame for a lot of it. Just go easy on him, at least until you know if he's behind this." I pointed at the note.

~~~

"What did you say to Jill?" Rob stopped me first thing the next morning. Greg hadn't been in to talk to him yet, so I figured he wasn't angry about that.

"Why? Did she call you?" I'd been hoping she'd leave me out of the conversation if she called him.

He nodded his head. "She called me last night."

"And?" I prompted when he didn't say anything else. He didn't look angry, but it could go either way depending on what she said to him.

"She wanted to know what really happened with Shirley. You're the only one that saw us. I figured she'd talked to you."

"She came to the tasting room on Sunday." His face darkened. "I didn't tell her anything," I added quickly. "I think she thought that we were dating, and I told her we weren't."
~~~

He shook his head. "Yeah, she accused me of having an affair with you as well as Shirley."

I gasped, taking a step back. "When she came to Sky Vineyards I told her there was nothing between us."

"I told her that too. She didn't believe either of us. She's the one that broke your car window, and she left a note telling your boyfriend he shouldn't trust you."

"She left that for Ty? Why would she do that?"

"Because she's not a nice person," he said. "When I first met her, she told me her father was rich, like that would be a turn-on. I have to admit it was, but she was always holding that over my head. As long as I did exactly what she wanted, she rewarded me with little gifts or money. When I did something she didn't like, she took back what she'd given me earlier."

He drew a deep breath, letting it out slowly. "I'm sorry for the way I've been acting. If you'll give me time to get some money saved, I'll pay to have that scratch on your car repaired."

"It's already taken care of. Don't worry about it. I'm just glad you found out what she was like before you married her. That wouldn't have been good for you."

"I'm not sure she ever planned on marrying me. She was angry at her father at the time we met. She was using me to get back at him. The engagement was her idea. Even the engagement ring came from her." He shook his head at his own stupidity. "She bought it herself. She just wanted someone to lead around by the nose."

"What are you going to do?"

"Nothing." He shrugged his shoulders. "She didn't want to get back together. She just wanted to accuse me of things I didn't do."

I patted his arm. "If you ask me, you dodged a bullet with her."

"You're probably right. It still stings to think I was so easily fooled. I don't think she's ever had an independent thought." He repeated what I'd told Skylar earlier.

"Until she can cut the apron strings, or whatever fathers use to bind their daughter to them, she will never be able to think for herself." I didn't think she would ever be able to cut those strings, but I didn't tell him that.

"Again, I'm sorry for what I did." Walking away, he looked like the weight of the world had been lifted off his shoulders.

~~~

He paced around the small room. He needed to get on with the game if he was going to make it work. The longer he put it off, the easier it was going to be for them to figure things out. That sheriff isn't exactly a country bumpkin. He hadn't followed the evidence he'd left behind.

He gave a frustrated sigh. Every now and then he questioned whether he would be able to pull this off. If the old man hadn't shown up, he could have gotten away with his scheme. Changing plans in the middle had seemed like a good idea, but now he wondered. Don't lose heart now, he told himself. He had to follow through. There was too much at stake to stop now. It was time to take the next step.
~~~

CHAPTER NINETEEN

"What did you do to Pattiann?" There was panic in the voice.

Hearing my name helped clear some of the fog clouding my brain. For a long moment I stayed still trying to figure out where I was and how I got there. The ground beneath me was hard. Grit dug into my bare legs. I didn't open my eyes. It sounded like two men were arguing. Their voices came to me as through a tunnel.

I tried to listen to what they were saying, but the words weren't making sense. My head felt like it was stuffed with dandelion fluff. "Don't worry about her. The worst she's going to suffer is a hangover headache." Had I gotten drunk? I didn't remember going out.

"If you hurt her, her brother is going to kill you." It was the same voice, Chase's voice. Was he arguing with himself? Is this what happened when the Dissociative Identity took command? I stayed still, listening, hoping to figure a way out of this. I needed to call Ty or Greg. My phone should be in my back pocket. I was lying on my side with my hands in front of me. If I moved enough to check for my phone, he'd notice. That didn't seem like a good idea at the moment.

"No one is going to kill me," Chase continued. "Well, not yet anyway. By then, we will have switched places. No one will know the difference."

My eyes sprung open at that, but I quickly shut them against the bright light that hit me in the face. Waiting another minute, I tried again, this time only opening them a small crack. Instinct told me to remain still so Chase wouldn't notice. I was in a warehouse of some sort. No, I was in a winery. I could see the barrels and vats. I wasn't at Sky Vineyards though. "Why did you bring her here? What are you going to do to her?"

"She's going to be fine. Stop worrying. Like I said, she'll

have a slight headache, nothing more. But I needed her here. She's going to help set the scene. You're going to rescue her from the evil brother. But by then, I'll be Chase, and you'll be Charles." The evil chuckle crawled over my skin. I didn't understand.

Who's Charles? Was that Chase's alter ego? I risked him noticing I was awake, and opened my eyes further. Two men were standing beside the barrel racks. I blinked my eyes hoping to clear the double vision. It looked like Chase was arguing with his own image in a mirror. But it wasn't an image. Another man, exactly like Chase, was standing there.

The piece of information I'd forgotten fell into place. At the diner, Chase said he had a brother. He'd left out the part about being twins. He didn't have Dissociative Identity Disorder.

As the fog began to lift from my mind, I remembered Chase had called me. He said he had something important to show me. He hadn't been on the porch when I arrived as I'd expected. Instead, he was standing in front of the building housing his winery. After that, everything was a blank. I couldn't remember anything else until I woke up a few minutes ago.

I was lying in an awkward position. My shoulder and hip were beginning to ache from lying on the hard concrete. Did I fall? Was something broken? I wiggled my fingers. They worked. Next I tried to move my arms without drawing the attention of the men. Everything seemed to be in working order, but even my thoughts were moving in slow motion. What the heck was going on? What had Chase, or Charles, done to me?

I continued to listen as the two men continued to argue.

"What's going on? Why are you doing this? Why are you even in Arizona?"

"You never were very sharp. I came here to take your place." He paused. "Well, that wasn't the original plan, but this will work just as well."

"What are you talking about?" My vision was still blurry, and I couldn't tell which man was speaking. Chase seemed as confused as I was.

"Why do you think? I'm tired of living in your shadow."

"My shadow? I haven't been around for a long time. Even when I was there, I didn't matter."

That must be Chase, I decided. I wasn't sure how I was going to keep them straight since they looked identical right down to the clothes they were wearing.

"You were his favorite," Chase continued. "You were the fair-haired boy that could do no wrong."

"Sure, I was his favorite," Charles scoffed. "I did everything he wanted. I gave up any dream I had to do whatever he wanted. He liked that, but he was obsessed with you. He was determined to bring you back to the fold. Why do you think he was trying to buy up the wineries around here? If he controlled the wineries, he thought you'd join the company as head of the wine division."

"I would never have agreed to that. What was your plan? Why were you trying to buy the wineries? I'll bet you weren't planning on turning them over to Dad."

"But I wasn't the one trying to buy them." Charles was smug now. "You were. If that damned lawyer had done his job right, you would already own several of those wineries."

"*You* hired the lawyer." He took a step towards his brother. "He came here demanding I pay him. I tried to tell him I hadn't hired him. I should have known it was you." Charles chuckled again, but didn't say anything. "How would this scheme benefit you?"

"Once your neighbors learned you had screwed them out of their businesses, they would have turned their backs on you. They wouldn't want anything to do with you. Father was ruthless, but he never cheated anyone. When he realized just how conniving you were, he'd no longer want you in the company."

"That doesn't make any more sense than what Dad was

planning. I never wanted anything to do with his company. Why would he think that changed now?" Chase shook his head.

"Whatever." The other man shrugged. "I came up with a better plan. The empire is still going to be mine, only I will be Chase, and you will be Charles."

"How do you think you're going to pull that off? I'm not going to stand silently by while you do that. People know me, they know who I am."

That evil chuckle sent chills up my spine again. "Really? That cute little gal I went out with didn't know the difference. She thought she was having dinner with Chase."

"You took Bonnie out posing as me," he accused. "Why did you tell her she couldn't work for me any longer? What was that supposed to accomplish?" He shook his head. "You aren't making any sense." I silently agreed with him. I was getting confused just listening to them.

"She just thought she was with Chase, only to find out later she was with Charles."

Chase shook his head again. "How will that help you?"

"When the smoke clears, I will explain to her that it wasn't me, Chase, she went out with. It was you, Charles. See how this is going to work?"

The real Chase shook his head. "No I don't. No one is going to believe you."

"Of course they will. People are so easily manipulated. They'll believe anything with the right evidence. I'll give them what they want to believe."

"What are you talking about?"

"Remember how we switched roles in high school? The girls never knew who they were dating." He laughed uproariously at the memory.

"That was never my idea, it was all on you," Chase argued. "I was never able to keep a girlfriend because of the tricks you played on them."

Charles lifted his shoulders in a shrug. "It doesn't matter.

It worked then, and it will work now. Here's how it's going to work. Charles, you," he pointed at Chase, "came over here to discredit Chase." This time he pointed at himself. "Unbeknownst to either of us, Dad came here to pull me back into the company. When Charles realized what he was up to, he had to stop him." He gave another shrug. "The only option open to you was to kill him."

His convoluted explanation was making my brain hurt, and I couldn't follow his logic.

"No one will believe that," Chase scoffed. "My friends know I would never do something like that."

"But it won't be you doing it. You're going to be Charles, remember?"

"You killed that woman, too. Why? Where did she fit into your plans?"

Charles shrugged. "It wasn't supposed to happen like that. But I suppose eventually it would have become necessary."

"Why? What did she do to you?"

"Did you know she was from Portland?" he answered. "She knew the Templeton name. I ran into her the day after she'd been in your tasting room. I'll bet you didn't even know she'd been there." He shook his head. "You always were such a dolt. Anyway, she naturally thought she was talking to Chase."

"That doesn't explain why you killed her."

"It was just innocent fun as long as she thought she was dating some big time vintner. When she remembered there were two of us, she wanted to know which one I was. She didn't believe me when I said I was Chase." He shook his head in confusion. "I don't know how she guessed," he said softly, distracted for a minute. "She thought she could get away with blackmailing me. I don't knuckle under to idle threats." His voice was a low growl now.

"Why did you bring Pattiann here?" He looked across the open space. I said a small prayer that they wouldn't be able to see that I was awake. My mind was still foggy, but I knew I wasn't meant to hear all of this.

"She's going to be my alibi, my witness."

"Witness to what? I'm never going to let you get away with this."

"Well, you won't have any say in the matter. You're going to be dead. Well, Charles is going to be dead. I had to kill Charles to save myself and that pretty little gal before he could kill us."

My soft gasp was loud enough to give me away. I couldn't believe he was going to kill his brother. But why not? He'd already killed his father and Shirley. What was one more? They turned as one to look at me. "Welcome to our party, Pattiann. You're awake a little sooner than I expected." I was pretty sure it was Charles who said that. This wasn't going to end well for me.

Before I could say anything, Chase struck out at his brother. Charles staggered back, but didn't go down. Lowering his head like a charging bull, he rammed into Chase. They both fell to the floor, continuing to strike out at each other. I thought I knew which one was Chase, but when the dust settled I didn't know which one came out on top.

One man was unconscious on the floor, the other rushed over to me. "Are you all right, Pattiann? Did he hurt you?"

I recoiled from his touch, unsure who he was. "Who are you?" It was a dumb question.

"I'm Chase." Of course he was going to say that. It was his plan to take Chase's place, so why not start now. "I'm sorry for what he did to you. To everyone," he added softly.

He sounded like Chase, but so did the other man. I looked at the inert figure on the floor. "Is that your twin brother?" Playing dumb wasn't hard at the moment. Fog slowed my thinking processes. Even after all that I'd heard I couldn't make sense of it.

"Yes," he sighed. "My evil twin. I can't believe what he's done." He took my arm to help me sit up. My skin crawled at his touch.

"I need to call Greg. Where's my phone?" I felt in my pockets, hoping it would be there.

My head felt the size of a hot air balloon as I sat up. The room spun. I reached out to touch my head, but couldn't even manage that much coordination. "What happened? What did you…he do to me?" If this was Charles, I needed to play along.

"Take it easy. Lie back down for a few minutes." Lying back on the hard floor, I felt like my eyes were spinning in their sockets. "How long have you been awake?" he asked. "How much did you hear?" Was that a hint of worry I detected in his voice.

"Something about Shirley. I don't know." I closed my eyes. Self-preservation told me to continue to play along. It didn't take much acting skills on my part.

"All right, just stay there for a few minutes while I tie him up."

"Wait. You have to call Greg."

"Don't worry, I'll call him. I'm going to tie him up first. We don't want him to get away, do we?" He tilted his head towards the crumpled figure across the room.

"No, of course not." Even I could hear the disappointment in my voice. "Are you the one that called me?" I asked from my position on the floor.

He shook his head. "It must have been Charles." The corners of his mouth lifted slightly. If he was Charles, he had no trouble remembering to switch names.

"How did he get my phone number?" The fog in my head was lifting, but I still wasn't thinking clearly. I remembered the mess in my spare room. If he was the one that had broken into my house, he could have gotten my cell phone number off an old bill. He didn't answer my question.

As he approached the figure across the room, the man reared up, hitting his brother with a hard right cross.

A startled grunt escaped the other man, and they grappled around for several minutes. One man was on the floor, the other was panting heavily as he came over to me. I wasn't sure of the outcome this time either.

"P-P-Pattiann, are you here?" Squinting into the bright spot light across the room, George shielded his eyes. "What d-d-did you d-d-do to her?" Rushing over to me, he fearlessly faced Chase. Or was it Charles? I didn't know.

"Who the hell are you?" the man snarled. Whoever this was, he didn't appreciate anyone interrupting him. He faced a furious George. The gentle giant had been replaced by the Incredible Hulk, and he was ready to tear someone apart.

"He's my friend," I said from my place on the floor. It still felt like my eyes were spinning in their sockets when I tried to sit up. I had no idea what he had given to me that made me feel like this.

Chase held out his hand towards George. "I'm glad you're here. You can help me." He pointed at the other man on the floor. "We need to tie him up so he won't get away. Can you do that?"

George looked from one man to the other, uncertainty playing across his face. "T-t-two of you?" He was as confused as I was. "You f-f-followed P-P-Pattiann."

"No, that wasn't me. It was him." He pointed to the man on the floor.

"Don't believe him. He's Charles," the crumpled figure said as he struggled to sit up. "He killed that woman, and his father, our father." Staggering to stand, the man stumbled across the open floor.

"Don't believe him." Again I was unsure who was speaking. "He's Charles, I'm Chase. Can't you see the difference? We really aren't alike." He turned to me. "You have to believe me, Pattiann. You know me." He stepped towards me, and I cringed away from him. Until I could figure out who I was talking to, I wasn't going to let either of them get close enough to grab me. One of them was a killer that much I was sure of.

I had no idea who was telling the truth. Either one of them

could be Chase, they looked that much alike. How would I be able to figure it out?

George stepped in front of me, his big body protecting me. "D-d-don't come c-c-closer," he stuttered. He held out his big hand to me, helping me stand up. He wasn't going to let anything happen to me. Still unsteady on my feet, I was able to stay upright with his help.

For several moments, I stared at the two men, so much alike, but so different. It was like being in a house of mirrors at a carnival. Both men claimed to be Chase. For now, I wanted to keep away from both of them. Until I could figure out which one was the real Chase, I'd call them Chase One and Chase Two. I figured the one who'd lost the fight had to be the real Chase. He was Chase One. Charles would fight harder. He had the most to lose since he'd killed two people.

"Are you okay, Pattiann?" Chase One asked. He didn't move closer, but I could feel the tension bottled up inside him.

"Stop pretending you care," Chase Two snapped. He turned to look at me. "Can't you see I'm Chase? You know me."

"It's not up to me to figure out who's who. We need to call Greg. Where's my cell phone?" I felt my pockets again.

Chase Two ignored me, appealing to George. "Help me tie him up, or he's going to get away."

Still holding George's hand, I took two steps towards the big doors urging him to follow me. If I could make it outside before the phony Chase stopped me, I'd be able to find my way to Sky Vineyards. Even in the dark, I knew the lay of the land better than he did. I had to get to Greg. Two people were already dead because of this guy, whichever one he was.

Before we had gone more than a few steps, Chase Two launched himself at his brother. "Come on, big guy," he called out to George. "Help me. We can't let him get away with murder."

Uncertain what he should do, George hesitated a second too long. The two men knocked into him, sending all three of them to the floor. George still held my hand as he went down. Staggering to stay upright, I barely managed to avoid joining them on the floor.

"R-r-run, P-P-Pattiann," George stammered.

I couldn't leave him here to face a killer alone. If Charles came out on top, I had no doubt that he would kill again. If he couldn't convince me that he was Chase, he would take me out along with George and his brother. Without a witness, he could claim he killed his brother in self-defense after he killed me and George. I was barely able to make sense out of my own whirling thoughts.

I looked around for something I could use as a weapon. Several boards were stacked against the wall. Lifting one, I wasn't sure I could get a good grip on the wide board to use it like a baseball bat. I took a couple of test swings. I might not be able to keep my grip on the board to do any damage, but I had to do something.

Please, God, direct my swing to the real killer, I whispered. *Don't let me hurt George or Chase.*

George was on the bottom of the pack. In the few minutes of my indecision, he had a split lip, and one eye was beginning to swell shut. He had a strong arm circled around the neck of each man. They weren't going to get away, but it didn't stop them from punching each other.

"Chase!" I shouted, hoping the real Chase would pause long enough for me to know it was him, not his brother.

With his arm drawn back preparing to throw another punch, he glanced at me. That was all I needed. I used my best softball stance and swing to bring the wide board around to connect with Charles's head. The board splintered making the impact less severe than I'd hoped. He was dazed, but not unconscious.

Shaking his head to rid himself of the stars he must be seeing, he tried to escape George's grip. George had no intention of letting go. He released the real Chase, pulling Charles into a headlock. He wasn't going anywhere. In the blink of an eye, the struggle was over.

Chase pulled his cell phone from his pocket. The cracked screen said he wasn't going to get service on it. I still didn't know what happened to mine. "The phone is back there." He pointed to the small room at the back of the building.

Within minutes, Greg's big SUV roared up in front of the building. Greg gathered me into a warm embrace before passing me off to Joe. He hugged me so tight I thought he was going to break my ribs, but I didn't care. It was over, and I was safe.

"Okay, George, you can let him go," Greg patted George's shoulder. He hesitated. His grip was locked in position unable to release the tension. "It's okay, George," Greg said softly. "He isn't going to get away."

George slowly relaxed his arm, and Charles fell forward, coughing and gasping. "That bastard tried to kill me," Charles squeaked. "You all saw that. I'm going to sue all of you." He turned to me. "Pattiann, how could you do this to me? You know I'm Chase. You're letting the real killer go." He pointed at his brother.

Chase lunged at him, but Greg prevented him from taking a swing. He already had the handcuffs on Charles. I prayed that it really was Charles I hit. Struggling against the restraint, he continued to claim he was Chase. Whether he really believed it, or he was trying to throw everyone into confusion was anyone's guess. I hoped there was some way Greg would eventually be able to prove which one was the real Chase Templeton.

George shook his head, trying to get something out around his split lip. "Sing-song, George, say it slow." Joe still had me in a vice-like grip. I wasn't even trying to get away.

"He followed Pattiann." George pointed at Charles. Giving his head a confused shake, he looked at Chase. "He's sort of like that guy." That's what he'd meant all along.

CHAPTER TWENTY

Between the paramedics coming to check out our injuries and giving our account of what happened, it was a very long night. Ty wasn't on duty, but he'd heard the call to Templeton Vineyard on his scanner. He beat the ambulance there. "What the hell happened?" He pulled me into his arms, shooting a dark glare at Chase.

Holding up his hands like he was warding off a blow, Chase took a step back. He didn't get a chance to explain. "It's that other guy," George pronounced, pointing at Charles where he was sitting on the floor with his hands cuffed behind his back. "They're sort of the same guy," George said, "but different." I wasn't sure how he knew which one had been following me.

Greg had discovered a syringe and a bottle of an animal sedative tucked into a gym bag tossed into a corner of the warehouse. I wasn't sure if they could pull fingerprints off the rough material of the bag, but maybe they would find one on the vial. I wanted proof-positive that they had the right man.

"You're going to have some memory loss," Ty said. He had reluctantly let the paramedics on duty examine me instead of doing it himself. He wanted me to go to the hospital, but I thought that was a little excessive. Other than the suggested memory loss and a slight headache, I was fine. George and Chase had more injuries than I did. They didn't want to go to the hospital either.

"I'm so sorry this happened," Chase said. The sky was just turning a pale pink when we all gathered in Mom's kitchen. For once, Greg and Joe weren't objecting to his presence. "I had no idea he was in town. He always enjoyed playing tricks on people with the twin thing. He always got away with it too," he added grudgingly.

"How did you find her?" Mom looked at George. She had insisted that he come with us, and was treating him like the hero he was. If he hadn't shown up when he did, I shuddered to think what Charles would have done.

He dipped his head, not looking at anyone. "I was following Pattiann to keep her safe." He remembered to use his sing-song voice to avoid the stutter. "I'm sorry I didn't obey your order, Sir." He looked up at Greg. "I knew something was wrong with that guy. I didn't know there were two of them."

"No one did, and I'm glad you didn't listen to me. You just might have saved her life and Chase's."

Mom had called Bonnie to let her know what happened, and Chase turned to her. "It wasn't me you went to dinner with that night. I hope you know I never would have said those things." He drew a deep breath, letting it out slowly. "I'm sorry he hurt you. I guess you won't be going out with me again anyway." He looked at Walt who had his arm around her. Walt had heard the 9-1-1 call too, and showed up minutes after the ambulance. "If you still want to work for me, I'd like that." I wasn't sure if his feelings were hurt or he was relieved.

"Is he the one who killed Shirley and your father?" she asked softly. Chase and I both nodded our heads. We'd heard what amounted to his confession.

Greg shrugged. "He's still claims we have the wrong guy, that he's Chase. Or maybe he's setting himself up for an insanity defense. Either way, it isn't going to work. His mother is sending his hair brush along with dental records. Their DNA might be identical, or close to it, because they're identical twins, but certain chemicals can be detected in the hair for several months. Chase has also provided the same from here. Charles won't be able to get out of the charges."

"My father was delusional if he thought he could bring me back into the business with the promise of becoming Vice-President of his new wine division," Chase said. "Working under his thumb would never work. I'm happy right where I am. My winery might be small potatoes in his estimation, but it's mine."

He drew a deep breath, letting it out slowly. "I never realized that choosing to go my own way had bothered him. In all the years I've been gone, I didn't know he was following what I've been able to do. It must have made him crazy to think I accomplished something without his input. He never gave either of us any credit for what we did. Anything we did, good or bad, was a reflection of him. He still thought he could buy me."

"What about your mother?" Mom turned to Chase. "What will she do with the business?"

Chase shrugged. "She's smart. She can run the company on her own if that's what she wants to do. If not, the Board of Directors can run it for her. This is where I'm staying. She knows that." Mom felt sorry for the woman she didn't know. She'd lost her husband and a son in the matter of days. Maybe getting back the one she'd lost years ago would help heal the wounds.

He drew a shaky breath. "She's welcome to come stay with me if that's what she wants. I was close to her when I was growing up, but she couldn't stand up to her husband. I hope she can have a life now."

I followed Ty outside as he got ready to leave a short time later. Leaning against his truck, he gathered me in his arms, his green eyes shining in the soft glow of the dawn. "I can't believe what you went through." His voice was hoarse with pent-up emotions. "That guy almost got away with murder. If you hadn't come around when you did, he might have killed Chase, putting his crimes on a dead man. No one would have been any the wiser."

"If George hadn't come in when he did, it could have been a lot worse," I added.

Placing his big hands on each side of my face, he drew me in for a tender kiss. "I thought my heart was going to stop when I heard that 9-1-1 call," he whispered before pulling me in for another kiss. When he finally lifted his head, he rested his forehead against mine, looking down at me. "With the murders cleared up, the guy following you in jail, and the flu season finally on the downside; do you think we might be able to spend a little more time together?"

I laughed, snuggling up against his hard body. "That sounds pretty good to me. What do you have in mind?"

He waggled his eyebrows suggestively. "We can start with dinner, just the two of us. We'll see what else we can come up with." It was a long time before either of us had anything more to say.

Since there was still sedative in my system, I called in sick. It wouldn't be safe for me to drive or take care of patients. There hadn't been time for Greg to talk to Rob about the note left on Ty's window. Rob wasn't behind that, so, I wasn't sure if he still wanted to talk to him. He might want to have a word with Jillian though.

I returned to work the following day, and everyone was treating George like a hero. As far as I was concerned, that's exactly what he was. Chase had offered him a job, but he was hoping to have his own handyman business someday. I thought there were a few people willing to see that happened sooner rather than later.

Midway through the morning, the dying wail of a siren announced the arrival of an ambulance. Illness and accidents didn't wait around for anyone. Ty came out of the back of the large vehicle, pulling a gurney with him. An oxygen mask obstructed our view of the elderly man's face.

"Mr. Maxwell has been sick for the past three days," Ty reported as he pushed the gurney through the doors. "It looks like the flu isn't through with us yet." He gave a frustrated sigh. We'd be putting in some extra hours again. We live to serve. I knew we'd find time for each other. It was still too early to say Ty was Mr. Right, but I was willing to take the necessary time to figure that out.

ACKNOWLEDGEMENTS

I thank God for answering my prayers and allowing me to write this book. I am so blessed by all He has given me. Without Him I can do nothing.

My thanks and gratitude also goes to KaTie Jackson, Gerry Beamon, and Sandy Roedl for their suggestions, editing and encouragement. I also want to thank Karyl Wilhelm of Wilhelm Family Vineyards for all her help with everything related to the vineyard and winery. Any mistakes or exaggerations are mine and not any fault of Karyl's.

Ken Shriner, a retired Phoenix Police Detective was kind enough to answer my questions regarding law enforcement. I'm grateful for his patience with me throughout the whole process. I've taken liberties with the way law enforcement works in an effort to move the story forward.

I'm most grateful to all of my fans. Thank you for your support and encouragement. I enjoy hearing from you.

OTHER BOOKS BY SUZANNE FLOYD

Revenge Served Cold
Rosie's Revenge
A Game of Cat and Mouse
Man on the Run
Trapped in a Whirlwind
Smoke & Mirrors
Plenty of Guilt
Lost Memories
Something Shady
Rosie's Secret
Killer Instincts
Never Con A Con Man
The Games People Play
Family Secrets
Picture That
Trading Places
Chasing His Shadow
Rosie's Legacy
Drawing Conclusions
Rosie's Texas Family
Back From The Grave
A Big Gamble
The Book Club Ladies
You'll Be Sorry
Family Is Everything
A Grave Decision
Payback or Justice

Dear Reader:

Thank you for reading my book. I hope you enjoyed reading it as much as I enjoyed writing it. If you enjoyed The Games People Play, I would appreciate it if you would tell your friends and relatives and/or write a review on Amazon. I hope you will also check out my other books at: Amazon.com

Like me on Facebook at Suzanne Floyd Author or check out my web page at Suzanne Floyd.com.

Thank you,
Suzanne Floyd

P.S. If you find any errors, please let me know at: Suzanne.sfloyd@gmail.com. Before publishing, many people have read the book, but minds can play tricks by supplying words that are missing and correcting typos.

Thanks again for reading my book.

ABOUT THE AUTHOR

Suzanne is an internationally known author. She was born in Iowa, and moved to Arizona with her family when she was nine years old where she still lives in Phoenix with her husband, Paul. They have two wonderful daughters, two great sons-in-law and five of the best grandchildren around. Of course, she is just a little prejudiced.

Growing up and traveling with her parents, she entertained herself by making up stories. As an adult she tried writing, but family came first. After retiring in 2008, she decided it was her time. She still enjoys making up stories, and thanks to the internet she's able to put them online for others to enjoy.

When Suzanne isn't writing, she and her husband enjoy traveling around on their 2010 Honda Goldwing trike. She's always looking for new places to write about. There's always a new mystery and a romance lurking out there to capture her attention.

www.ingramcontent.com/pod-product-compliance
Lightning Source LLC
LaVergne TN
LVHW010058170826
845678LV00012B/2166

* 9 7 8 1 7 1 7 9 1 3 6 1 6 *